SCHOLASTIC INC.

Published by Scholastic Inc., *Publishers since 1920*. SCHOLASTIC and associated logos are trademarks and/or registered trademarks of Scholastic Inc.

ISBN 978-1-338-05831-4
10 9 8 7 6 5 4 3 2 1 17 18 19 20 21

Printed in the U.S.A. 40
First printing 2017

THE WORLD OF YO-KAI!

Unexplained occurrences happen every day, but if you possess the Yo-kai Watch, you will have the amazing and rare ability to see the elusive Yo-kai—invisible beings responsible for life's daily annoyances. But beware . . . when a Yo-kai enters your life, things will never be quite the same.

That's exactly what happened to Nate Adams. One summer day, he went out on a bug-hunting adventure with his friends. Deep in the woods of Mount Wildwood, Nate stumbled upon something strange: the Crank-a-kai, an ancient stone capsule machine.

When Nate inserted a coin into the mysterious machine, a capsule popped out—and Nate encountered something really extraordinary. As he opened the capsule, a bolt of light shot out into the sky—*WHOOSH!* Suddenly, floating right in front of him was a supernatural being—a Yo-kai named Whisper.

At first, Nate didn't want any part of the machine's prize or the annoying, ghostlike being inside it. But Whisper was persistent, and in the end, Nate finally accepted the honor that had been bestowed upon him—insight into the world of Yo-kai.

WHAT ARE YO-KAI?

Yo-kai are supernatural beings that live in a dimension parallel to the human world. They often come to the human realm and influence people in all kinds of strange and mysterious ways.

Yo-kai usually don't want to hurt anyone; they just love pranks and causing mayhem. When a Yo-kai "inspirits" a person, the Yo-kai takes total control of the person's body and makes them do and say things they don't mean to—sometimes playfully, and sometimes NOT so playfully.

The only way to stop a Yo-kai is by negotiation or confrontation. But first you have to see where they are. The problem is, Yo-kai are invisible. No one can see them without the watch. And the most effective way for Nate to battle them is with the help of the Yo-kai he's already befriended.

How you approach each Yo-kai in battle depends on which of the eight tribes they belong to. Each Yo-kai belongs to a different tribe depending on his or her personality.

To learn more about each tribe, turn the page . . .

SUMMONING

CHARMING

Alarming! Boom-boom walla-walla dance-dance Charming!

They may look super cute and cuddly, but these Yo-kai can still totally take care of business! Komasan, Jibanyan, and Komajiro belong to Charming.

SUMMONING

Sumo shave, flavo engrave, flash team'a Brave!

BRAVE

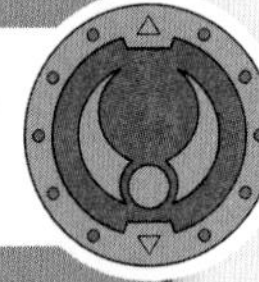

The cool, courageous Brave Yo-kai excel at combat and are forces to be reckoned with! Blazion, B3-NK1, Sheen, and Shogunyan belong to Brave.

SUMMONING

TOUGH *Gruff stuff, rough bluff, red ban jacket stand bling blang Tough!*

Don't mess with these Yo-kai! They are tough inside and out, and they're all about strong defense. Noway, Robonyan, Roughraff, and Fidgephant belong to Tough.

SUMMONING

Boo-shiggy boo-shiggy boogie-woogies! Cling-clang delirious Mysterious! **MYSTERIOUS**

With their eccentric looks and odd behavior, these strange and unpredictable Yo-kai will leave you guessing! Tattletell, Tengu, Signibble, and Kyubi belong to Mysterious.

SUMMONING

HEARTFUL

Speedy artful, sing la-la-la, everywhere Heartful!

These gentle, warmhearted Yo-kai are at their best when they are healing or helping you relax. Hungramps, Happierre, Enerfly, and Wiglin, Steppa, and Rhyth belong to Heartful.

SUMMONING

Lookie lee lookie lee flippidy dee! Lookie lee lookie lee bubba Eerie!

EERIE

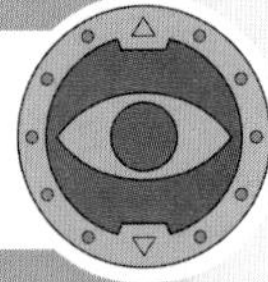

The weird and creepy-looking Eerie Yo-kai will make you shiver in your boots! Manjimutt, Cheeksqueek, Dismarelda, and Rockabelly belong to Eerie.

SUMMONING

SHADY

Marvelous thee! Gutsy, free banshee! Sing, song Shady!

These gloomy Yo-kai prefer to mope and withdraw to the dark shadows. Watch out or they will drag you right down with them! Hidabat, Timidevil, Dimmy, and Tengloom all belong to Shady.

SUMMONING

SLIPPERY

Trippery! Gippery! Slimey wimey do Slippery!

The Slippery Yo-kai prefer to go their own way and are really, really hard to get ahold of! Venoct, Noko, Dragon Lord, and Cynake belong to Slippery.

RARE YO-KAI

Rare Yo-kai are very hard to come by. In all his adventures, Nate has been fortunate to meet two rare Yo-kai—Robonyan and Peppillon.

And then there's the really rare Dianyan, Sapphinyan, Emenyan, Rubinyan, Goldenyan, and Topanyan. Very, very little is known about these Yo-kai!

LEGENDARY YO-KAI

***Imaginary, incendiary!
Flip flap squiggle boom
slim slam Legendary!***

When you collect a certain number of Yo-kai Medals, you may unlock a seal that summons a Legendary Yo-kai! Not much is actually known about Legendary Yo-kai. They are very powerful and the rarest of the rare Yo-kai.

After collecting eight Yo-kai Medals, Nate met Shogunyan, the Yo-kai of Jibanyan's ancestor. When his first Yo-kai Medallium was filled, Nate met Dandoodle, a type of Manjimutt.

THE YO-KAI WATCH

On that fateful day in the woods, Whisper gave Nate a Yo-kai Watch that lets him see all the hidden Yo-kai. But more importantly, the watch granted Nate the ability to see all the mischief the Yo-kai cause in his hometown of Springdale.

When Nate presses the button on the side of the Yo-kai Watch, it lights up and reveals any Yo-kai lurking nearby.

YO-KAI WATCH MODEL ZERO

After many adventures with the original Yo-kai Watch, Nate and Whisper hear about a new and updated version. The famous inventor Steve Jaws reveals the Yo-kai Watch Model Zero, which he describes as "new but familiar, reassuring yet revolutionary—a watch that will bridge the worlds between Yo-kai and humans." The new watch can do a super summon using special Z medals. Now Nate can switch back and forth between the watches using Whisper!

YO-KAI MEDALS

Once Nate befriends a Yo-kai, he or she gives him a medal as a symbol of their friendship. Nate can use the Yo-kai Medal to summon his new friend whenever he needs help. With so many mischievous Yo-kai out in the world, Nate is constantly calling on his Yo-kai friends to solve life's everyday problems.

THE YO-KAI MEDALLIUM

Once Nate earned his first eight Yo-kai Medals, Whisper gave Nate the Yo-kai Medallium to keep them in a safe place. It was a much more respectful way to honor his Yo-kai friends than Nate's first choice—shoving them inside a random drawer in his room.

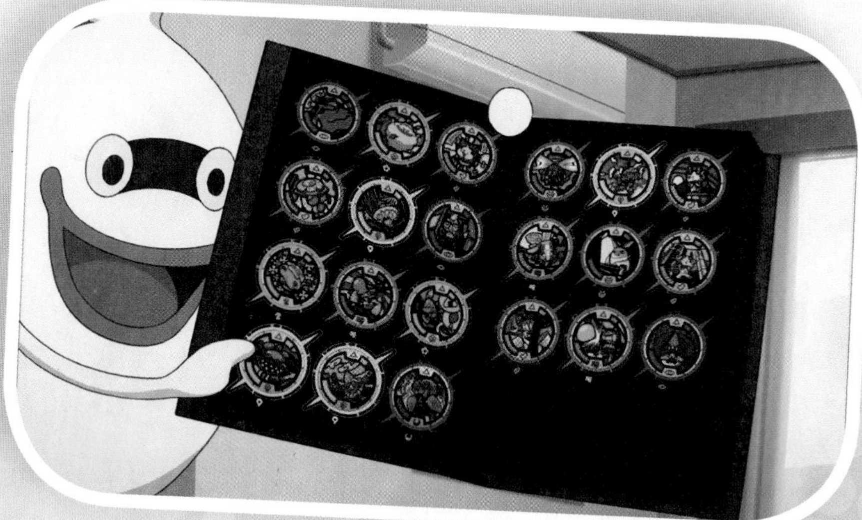

NATE

NAME:
Nathan (Nate) Adams

GRADE: 5

FRIENDS:
Bear, Eddie, and Katie

BEST YO-KAI FRIEND:
Jibanyan

SCHOOL:
Springdale Elementary

CATCHPHRASE: "Yo-kai Medal, do your thing!"

STATS

Nate is a pretty ordinary fifth grader. He doesn't excel at anything except being completely average. But average is the last thing that Nate wants to be.

TRIBE: ??

ABILITIES: Guide (sort of)

CATCHPHRASE: "What's up, my corporeal friend?"

OCCUPATION: Self-proclaimed Yo-kai butler

STATS

WHISPER

One hundred and ninety years ago, Whisper was locked in an ancient stone capsule machine by a group of monks who declared him a menace to society. Now, as Nate's self-proclaimed "Yo-kai butler," Whisper is determined to help Nate solve his problems and learn more about Yo-kai—whether Nate wants to or not!

WHISPER'S YO-KAI PAD

This digital encyclopedia of the Yo-kai has been very important in Nate's confrontations with Yo-kai. Whisper loves to go on and on about his Yo-kai knowledge, but he only has that knowledge because he's constantly referring back to his Yo-kai Pad.

HOW TO USE THIS BOOK

Ready to learn the facts about your favorite Yo-kai? Here's a rundown on just what you'll discover.

CATCHPHRASE
It's what a Yo-kai can be heard saying over and over and over again!

SEASON
This tells you which season of the animation each Yo-kai appears in. Season 1 includes episodes 1-26. Season 2 includes episodes 27-76.

NUMBER
This is the Yo-kai's Medallium entry number.

TRIBE
Each Yo-kai belongs to one of the eight Yo-kai Tribes. The Yo-kai's personality determines the tribe that he or she belongs to.

YO-KAI NAME
Names often reveal something fun and funny about the Yo-kai's personality.

DESCRIPTION
This snapshot of the Yo-kai will help you as you confront and negotiate your way to defeating and hopefully befriending each Yo-kai you encounter.

NUMBER
1
BRAVE
PANDLE
TV SEASON 2
A careless Yo-kai who makes other people just as careless! He enters battle wearing only a loincloth . . . and a pan . . . on his head. Try not to take after him so much.
SKILL: Careless
ATTACK: Pesky Poke
SOULTIMATE MOVE: Pointy Toothpick
INSPIRIT: Careless
TECHNIQUE: Fire
FAVORITE FOOD: Rice Balls
EASINESS TO BEFRIEND:
CATCHPHRASE: "Gotcha!"
STATS
EVOLUTION: NO EVOLUTIONS
FUSION: NO FUSIONS
NUMBER
2
BRAVE
SKILL: Careless
ATTACK: Pointy Pokes
SOULTIMATE MOVE: Toothpick Rainfall
INSPIRIT: Defenseless
TECHNIQUE: Fire
FAVORITE FOOD: Rice Balls
EASINESS TO BEFRIEND:
UNDY
EVOLUTION:
Pandle level 18
Undy
20

SKILL
This special natural ability that Yo-kai automatically use in battle can be offensive or defensive.

ATTACK
When a Yo-kai physically attacks, he or she uses an offensive move. The power of the attack can range from multiple lightweight hits to one powerful knockdown hit.

SOULTIMATE MOVE
In battle, when a Yo-kai's Soul Meter is full, the Yo-kai can use his or her Soultimate Move—a special signature move—against the Yo-kai opponent. Each one is unique and has varying levels of boost effect and damage.

EVOLUTION
If a Yo-kai has the ability to evolve into a more powerful being with a different name and appearance, it will happen automatically once the Yo-kai hits a specific level.

INDEX
Need to find a Yo-kai but not sure what his or her number is? Turn to the handy index that begins on page 188. The index lists all the Yo-kai alphabetically to help you find the one you're looking for.

MEDAL
Each Yo-kai's Medal is a symbol of their friendship. The medal has a picture of the Yo-kai and reveals what tribe he or she belongs to. Medals for Legendary Yo-kai have gold frames.

GLEAM
RARE! A holy swordsman with a divine blade that cuts through evil like cheddar cheese. Could he bring about tasty world peace?
RARE!
STATS
SKILL: Light Speed
ATTACK: Lightning Slash
SOULTIMATE MOVE: Holy Slash
INSPIRIT: Holy Sword
TECHNIQUE: Shock
FAVORITE FOOD: Seafood
EASINESS TO BEFRIEND: —
EVOLUTION: NO EVOLUTIONS
FUSION:
Chansin + Holy Blade = Gleam
33

RARE!
Some Yo-kai are harder to find than others. These Yo-kai are considered Rare.

TECHNIQUE
Every Yo-kai can use their specific elemental-based power to attack or heal as much as possible during battle.

FAVORITE FOOD
This is a Yo-kai's favorite food to eat during battle. If you give a Yo-kai his or her favorite food, you increase your chance of befriending the Yo-kai.

EASINESS TO BEFRIEND
The more stars a Yo-kai has, the easier it is to befriend after you've defeated him or her. If a Yo-kai has no stars, that means he or she is almost impossible to befriend.

INSPIRIT
When a Yo-kai takes over, this is how they infect whoever they are inspiriting. It doesn't always have a negative effect. Sometimes it can actually have a positive one.

FUSION
Certain Yo-kai can fuse with another Yo-kai or item and, in turn, create a brand-new, more powerful being.

MEET THE YO-KAI

NUMBER 1

BRAVE

PANDLE

TV SEASON 2

A careless Yo-kai who makes other people just as careless! He enters battle wearing only a loincloth . . . and a pan . . . on his head. Try not to take after him so much.

STATS

SKILL: Careless

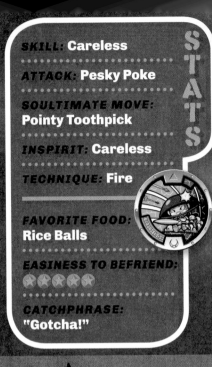

ATTACK: Pesky Poke

SOULTIMATE MOVE: Pointy Toothpick

INSPIRIT: Careless

TECHNIQUE: Fire

FAVORITE FOOD: Rice Balls

EASINESS TO BEFRIEND: ★★★★★

CATCHPHRASE: "Gotcha!"

EVOLUTION: NO EVOLUTIONS **FUSION:** NO FUSIONS

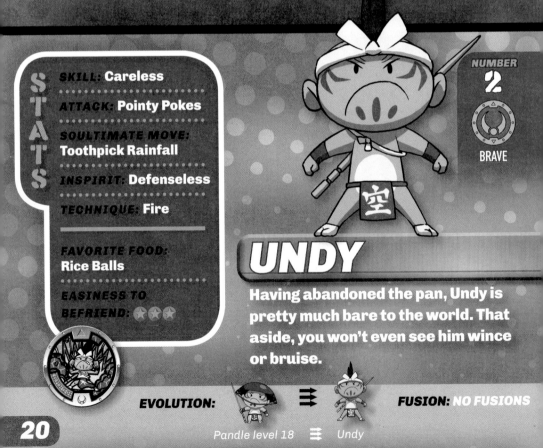

STATS

SKILL: Careless

ATTACK: Pointy Pokes

SOULTIMATE MOVE: Toothpick Rainfall

INSPIRIT: Defenseless

TECHNIQUE: Fire

FAVORITE FOOD: Rice Balls

EASINESS TO BEFRIEND: ★★★

NUMBER 2

BRAVE

UNDY

Having abandoned the pan, Undy is pretty much bare to the world. That aside, you won't even see him wince or bruise.

EVOLUTION:    **FUSION:** NO FUSIONS

Pandle level 18 ⇛ Undy

NUMBER

3

BRAVE

TANBO

RARE! A Yo-kai who is always first to the battle! With nothing to slow him down, he shows up early and always has a nice tan.

RARE!

先

STATS

SKILL: Careless

ATTACK: Pointy Pokes

SOULTIMATE MOVE: Gutsy Cut

INSPIRIT: Gutsiness

TECHNIQUE: Pebble

FAVORITE FOOD: Rice Balls

EASINESS TO BEFRIEND: ★★★

EVOLUTION: NO EVOLUTIONS * **FUSION:** NO FUSIONS

NUMBER
4

BRAVE

CUTTA-NAH

A lazy katana Yo-kai who can drain you of all your motivation. He's strangely sharp for being so lazy.

STATS

SKILL: Bladed Body

ATTACK: Double Slice

SOULTIMATE MOVE: Halfhearted Chop

INSPIRIT: Aimless

TECHNIQUE: Whirlwind

FAVORITE FOOD: Juice

EASINESS TO BEFRIEND: ★★★★

EVOLUTION: NO EVOLUTIONS * **FUSION:** NO FUSIONS

STATS

SKILL: Bladed Body

ATTACK: Double Slice

SOULTIMATE MOVE: Resigned Rush

INSPIRIT: Laziness

TECHNIQUE: Whirlwind

FAVORITE FOOD: Juice

EASINESS TO BEFRIEND: ★★★

NUMBER
5

BRAVE

CUTTA-NAH-NAH

Too lazy to get a haircut, but not too lazy to slash enemies with his untidy strands.

EVOLUTION:   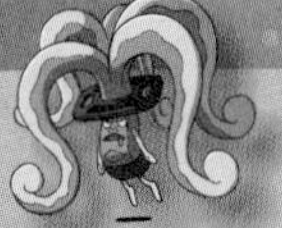

Cutta-nah level 20 ⇛ Cutta-nah-nah

FUSION: NO FUSIONS

NUMBER 6

BRAVE

SLACKA-SLASH

RARE!

RARE! More dangerous than he looks, Slacka-slash can beat his foes with only a single slice.

STATS

SKILL: Bladed Body

ATTACK: Double Slice

SOULTIMATE MOVE: Phantom Smash

INSPIRIT: Laziness

TECHNIQUE: Hail

FAVORITE FOOD: Juice

EASINESS TO BEFRIEND: 

EVOLUTION: NO EVOLUTIONS ✱ **FUSION:** NO FUSIONS

NUMBER

7

BRAVE

TV SEASON 2

MOCHISMO

He's cute most of the time, but when he's mad, his body cracks and his manly face pops out.

STATS

SKILL: Soft Skin

ATTACK: Power Punch

SOULTIMATE MOVE: Mochi Punch

INSPIRIT: Mochi Power

TECHNIQUE: Pebble

FAVORITE FOOD: Rice Balls

EASINESS TO BEFRIEND: ★★★★★

EVOLUTION: NO EVOLUTIONS * **FUSION:** NO FUSIONS

STATS

SKILL: Soft Skin

ATTACK: Power Punch

SOULTIMATE MOVE: Minochi Punch

INSPIRIT: Jealousy

TECHNIQUE: Fire

FAVORITE FOOD: Rice Balls

EASINESS TO BEFRIEND: ★★★★

NUMBER

8

BRAVE

MINOCHI

When he's in love, he gets overly protective about his partner. He can make you a very jealous person.

EVOLUTION: NO EVOLUTIONS * **FUSION:** NO FUSIONS

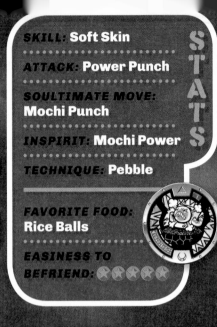

HELMSMAN

A floating helmet that was worn by a famous military commander. It spends its days searching for its body—a good use of time.

STATS

SKILL: Spirit Guard

ATTACK: Headbutt

SOULTIMATE MOVE: Helmsman Helm

INSPIRIT: Helmet Defense

TECHNIQUE: Shock

FAVORITE FOOD: Vegetables

EASINESS TO BEFRIEND: ★★★

EVOLUTION: NO EVOLUTIONS * **FUSION:** NO FUSIONS

STATS

SKILL: Spirit Guard

ATTACK: Stab Storm

SOULTIMATE MOVE: Knight's Slash

INSPIRIT: Knight's Curse

TECHNIQUE: Shock

FAVORITE FOOD: Vegetables

EASINESS TO BEFRIEND: ★★

REUKNIGHT

Helmsman and Armsman reunited. He now aspires to do what he couldn't do when he was alive—unify the country.

EVOLUTION: NO EVOLUTIONS * **FUSION:**

 +  = 

Helmsman + Armsman = Reuknight

RARE!

CORPTAIN

NUMBER 11

BRAVE

RARE! A popular leader when he was alive, Corptain leads an army of souls even after death. Now that's charisma!

STATS

SKILL: Spirit Guard

ATTACK: Stab Storm

SOULTIMATE MOVE: Ticket to Hades

INSPIRIT: Stygian Curse

TECHNIQUE: Absorb

FAVORITE FOOD: Vegetables

EASINESS TO BEFRIEND: 

EVOLUTION: NO EVOLUTIONS * **FUSION:** NO FUSIONS

BLAZION

IN THE VIDEO GAME:

The king of beasts with a mane of fire! This hot-blooded Yo-kai fills folks with fiery enthusiasm.

IN THE ANIMATION:

Go for the gold! Push it to the limit! This feisty little Yo-kai makes people feel super motivated. He even made Nate volunteer to scrub toilets! Gross!

STATS

SKILL: **Blazing Spirit**

ATTACK: **Practiced Punch**

SOULTIMATE MOVE: **Blazing Fist**

INSPIRIT: **Emblaze**

TECHNIQUE: **Blaze**

CATCHPHRASE: **"Rawr, roar, rawr!"**

FAVORITE FOOD: **Meat**

EASINESS TO BEFRIEND: ★★★★

EVOLUTION: ***NO EVOLUTIONS***

FUSION: ***NO FUSIONS***

RARE!

QUAKEN

RARE! Every step Quaken takes shakes everything around him . . . and some of those vibrations can even move your heart. Awwwwww!

STATS

SKILL: Courageous Spirit

ATTACK: Practiced Punch

SOULTIMATE MOVE: Earthshaker

INSPIRIT: Lion's Pride

TECHNIQUE: Rockslide

FAVORITE FOOD: Meat

EASINESS TO BEFRIEND: 

EVOLUTION: NO EVOLUTIONS * **FUSION:** NO FUSIONS

NUMBER
14

BRAVE

SIRO

RARE! **Siro brings out the best in those he inspirits. They become shining lights for the future.**

RARE!

STATS

SKILL: Shining Spirit

ATTACK: Practiced Punch

SOULTIMATE MOVE: Roaring Stance

INSPIRIT: Heart's Roar

TECHNIQUE: Lightning

FAVORITE FOOD: Meat

EASINESS TO BEFRIEND: 

EVOLUTION: NO EVOLUTIONS * **FUSION:** NO FUSIONS

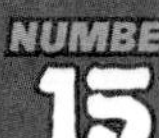

15

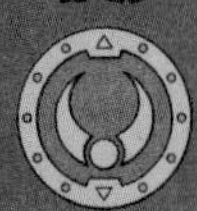

BRAVE

CHANSIN

Once a proud warrior, Chansin threw it all away by gambling . . . Now his best odds are to retreat.

STATS

SKILL: **Gambler**

ATTACK: **One-Two Punch**

SOULTIMATE MOVE: **Go for Broke**

INSPIRIT: **Bad Bet**

TECHNIQUE: **Fire**

FAVORITE FOOD: **Seafood**

EASINESS TO BEFRIEND: ★★★

EVOLUTION: ***NO EVOLUTIONS*** ✱ ***FUSION:*** ***NO FUSIONS***

NUMBER
16

SHEEN

BRAVE

A Yo-kai swordsman who returned to the way of the sword when a legendary blade reignited his spirit.

STATS

SKILL: Light Speed

ATTACK: Lightning Slash

SOULTIMATE MOVE: Legendary Slash

INSPIRIT: Fine Weapon

TECHNIQUE: Whirlwind

FAVORITE FOOD: Seafood

EASINESS TO BEFRIEND:

EVOLUTION:
NO EVOLUTIONS

FUSION:

+

=

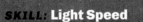

Chansin + Legendary Blade = Sheen

BRAVE

SNEE

Cursed by his demon blade, Snee searches the world for blood. He excels at silently sneaking up on his enemies.

STATS

SKILL: Cursed Skin

ATTACK: Lightning Slash

SOULTIMATE MOVE: Demonic Slash

INSPIRIT: Cursed Sword

TECHNIQUE: Absorb

FAVORITE FOOD: Seafood

EASINESS TO BEFRIEND: ★★★

EVOLUTION: NO EVOLUTIONS * **FUSION:**

Chansin + Cursed Blade = Snee

GLEAM

RARE!

RARE! A holy swordsman with a divine blade that cuts through evil like cheddar cheese. Could he bring about tasty world peace?

SKILL: Light Speed

ATTACK: Lightning Slash

SOULTIMATE MOVE: Holy Slash

INSPIRIT: Holy Sword

TECHNIQUE: Shock

FAVORITE FOOD: Seafood

EASINESS TO BEFRIEND: —

EVOLUTION: NO EVOLUTIONS ✱ **FUSION:**

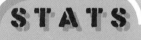

Chansin + Holy Blade = Gleam

NUMBER 19

BRAVE

BENKEI

Hiding 999 weapons from fallen foes in his stomach, Benkei can call any one of them in a moment of need.

STATS

SKILL: Sword Hunting

ATTACK: Lightning Slash

SOULTIMATE MOVE: 999 Blades

INSPIRIT: Clumsiness

TECHNIQUE: Hail

FAVORITE FOOD: Chinese Food

EASINESS TO BEFRIEND: ★★★

EVOLUTION: NO EVOLUTIONS
FUSION: NO FUSIONS

NUMBER 20

BRAVE

TV SEASON 1

B3-NK1

STATS

SKILL: Sword Hunting

ATTACK: Lightning Slash

SOULTIMATE MOVE: B3-NK1 GUN

INSPIRIT: Cyborg Strength

TECHNIQUE: Shock

FAVORITE FOOD: Chinese Food

EASINESS TO BEFRIEND: ★★

EVOLUTION: NO EVOLUTIONS
FUSION: NO FUSIONS

IN THE VIDEO GAME:

A Yo-kai whose body is half machine. It could very well be the world's first cyborg Yo-kai.

IN THE ANIMATION:

B3-NK1 is a powerful robot that breaks machines and steals the screws. When he collects 1,000 screws, his mighty sword will be unstoppable.

SUSHIYAMA

BRAVE

A Yo-kai who desperately wants to be Japanese. He sleeps on a futon and only eats sushi. I think he might be doing it wrong . . .

STATS

SKILL: Guard Break

ATTACK: Headbuster

SOULTIMATE MOVE: Sushiyama Strike

INSPIRIT: Samurai Spirit

TECHNIQUE: Hail

FAVORITE FOOD: Rice Balls

EASINESS TO BEFRIEND: ★★★★

EVOLUTION: NO EVOLUTIONS * **FUSION:** NO FUSIONS

RARE!

NUMBER 22

BRAVE

KAPUNKI

RARE! A punk Yo-kai who wears kabuki-style makeup. He dreams of rocking the socks and faces off his fans all across the globe.

STATS

SKILL: The Stand

ATTACK: Headbuster

SOULTIMATE MOVE: Boastful Bomber

INSPIRIT: Kabuki Fun

TECHNIQUE: Fire

FAVORITE FOOD: Rice Balls

EASINESS TO BEFRIEND: 

EVOLUTION: NO EVOLUTIONS ✱ **FUSION:** NO FUSIONS

NUMBER 23

BRAVE

BEETLER

Beetler is a young battler who fights with his horns and his fists. He trains with his rival, Rhinoggin.

STATS

SKILL: Too Serious

ATTACK: One-Two Punch

SOULTIMATE MOVE: Big Pincers

INSPIRIT: Stag Power

TECHNIQUE: Pebble

FAVORITE FOOD: Vegetables

EASINESS TO BEFRIEND: ★★★

EVOLUTION: NO EVOLUTIONS ✻ **FUSION:** NO FUSIONS

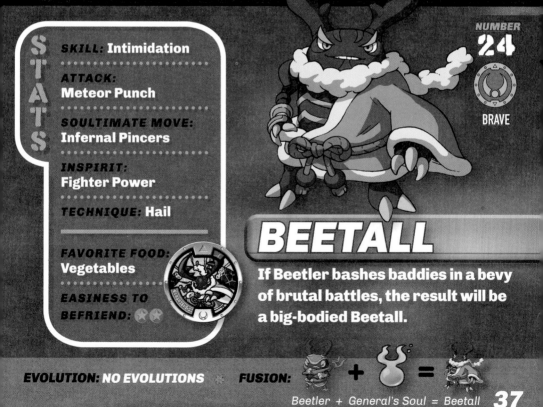

NUMBER 24

BRAVE

BEETALL

If Beetler bashes baddies in a bevy of brutal battles, the result will be a big-bodied Beetall.

STATS

SKILL: Intimidation

ATTACK: Meteor Punch

SOULTIMATE MOVE: Infernal Pincers

INSPIRIT: Fighter Power

TECHNIQUE: Hail

FAVORITE FOOD: Vegetables

EASINESS TO BEFRIEND: ★★

EVOLUTION: NO EVOLUTIONS ✻ **FUSION:**

Beetler + General's Soul = Beetall

RARE!

NUMBER
25

BRAVE

CRUNCHA

RARE! A stag beetle Yo-kai who represents the apex of the thorax. He can grant you incredible strength.

STATS

SKILL: Intimidation

ATTACK: Meteor Punch

SOULTIMATE MOVE: The Guillotine

INSPIRIT: Legend Power

TECHNIQUE: Lightning

FAVORITE FOOD: Vegetables

EASINESS TO BEFRIEND: —

EVOLUTION: NO EVOLUTIONS * **FUSION:** NO FUSIONS

ZERBERKER

Legend has it that this Yo-kai leveled an entire village with one tantrum. You'll explode with rage if he's around.

STATS

SKILL: **Annoyance**

ATTACK: **Lightning Slash**

SOULTIMATE MOVE: **Zerberker Slash**

INSPIRIT: **Berserk**

TECHNIQUE: **Fire**

FAVORITE FOOD: **Meat**

EASINESS TO BEFRIEND: ★★

EVOLUTION: NO EVOLUTIONS ***FUSION: NO FUSIONS***

RARE!

NUMBER
27

SNARTLE

BRAVE

RARE! This Yo-kai visits homes asking, "Any brats here?" It's a way of scaring kids into behaving . . . kind of like a reverse Santa.

TV SEASON 2

STATS

SKILL: Sword Hunting

ATTACK: Lightning Slash

SOULTIMATE MOVE: For Naughty Brats

INSPIRIT: Frighten

TECHNIQUE: Hail

FAVORITE FOOD: Meat

EASINESS TO BEFRIEND: 

EVOLUTION: NO EVOLUTIONS * **FUSION:** NO FUSIONS

NUMBER 28

MYSTERIOUS

SNOTSOLONG

A crane Yo-kai with an insanely runny nose. He's scared his drippings will make him too heavy to fly. I'd be scared, too.

STATS

SKILL: Water Play

ATTACK: Pesky Poke

SOULTIMATE MOVE: Stretchy Slap

INSPIRIT: Runny Nose

TECHNIQUE: Torrent

FAVORITE FOOD: Seafood

EASINESS TO BEFRIEND: ★★★★★

EVOLUTION: NO EVOLUTIONS
FUSION: NO FUSIONS

NUMBER 29

MYSTERIOUS

DUCHOO

TV SEASON 1

STATS

SKILL: Snow Play

ATTACK: Pesky Poke

SOULTIMATE MOVE: Sneezy Spike

INSPIRIT: Catch Cold

TECHNIQUE: Frost

CATCHPHRASE: *Sniffing*

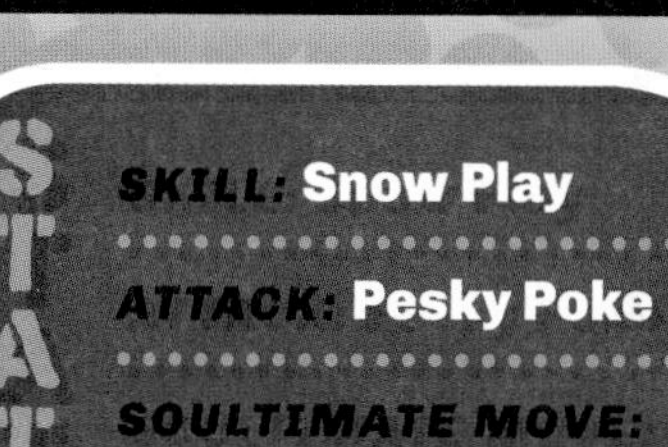

FAVORITE FOOD: Seafood

EASINESS TO BEFRIEND: ★★★★

IN THE VIDEO GAME:

Ever felt like you might be sick, but you're not sure if you really are? Blame Duchoo.

IN THE ANIMATION:

If a kid wishes really, really, really, super, super, duper hard to skip school, then Duchoo will maybe show up. Nate summoned Duchoo once, but his mom didn't fall for it.

EVOLUTION: NO EVOLUTIONS
FUSION: NO FUSIONS

NUMBER 30

MYSTERIOUS

WAZZAT

TV SEASONS 1 AND 2

SKILL: Forgot to Defend

ATTACK: Bite

SOULTIMATE MOVE: Wuwuzzat?

INSPIRIT: Memory Eater

TECHNIQUE: Whirlwind

CATCHPHRASE: "Ignorance is bliss."

FAVORITE FOOD: Candy

EASINESS TO BEFRIEND:

IN THE VIDEO GAME:

It fits snugly on your head before it devours your memories. It can be nice to forget the bad ones . . . or to just wear a hat.

IN THE ANIMATION:

Wazzat makes you feel scatterbrained. After he erased one of Nate's most embarrassing moments, Wazzat got really carried away.

EVOLUTION: NO EVOLUTIONS

FUSION: NO FUSIONS

SKILL: Prediction

ATTACK: Bite

SOULTIMATE MOVE: Ignorance Is Bliss

INSPIRIT: Liven Up

TECHNIQUE: Shock

FAVORITE FOOD: Candy

EASINESS TO BEFRIEND:

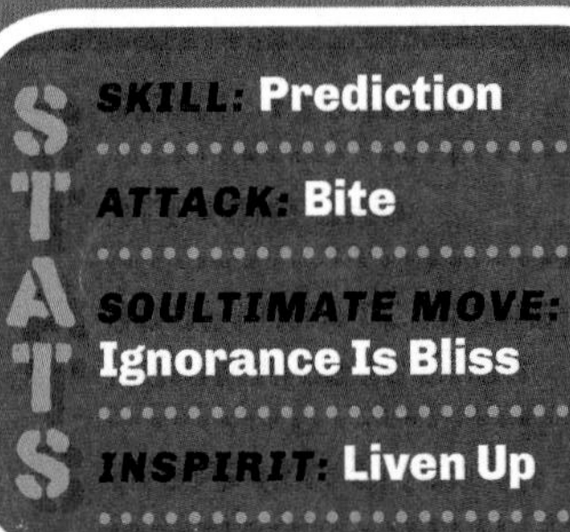

TV SEASON 2

NUMBER 31

MYSTERIOUS

DUMMKAP

This hat Yo-kai can make geniuses into dreamy fools. A foolish life can be more fun . . . but would you even realize if it was?!

EVOLUTION: NO EVOLUTIONS ✱ FUSION: NO FUSIONS

D'WANNA

IN THE VIDEO GAME:

D'wanna's chants will weaken your resolve! This can make you give up on . . . y'know, stuff and whatever.

IN THE ANIMATION:

D'wanna makes people quit whatever they're doing, which leads to a lot of unused gym memberships and bridges to nowhere..

STATS

SKILL: Soothing Rhythm

ATTACK: Hit

SOULTIMATE MOVE: Croaking Prayer

INSPIRIT: Full of Sighs

TECHNIQUE: Heal

CATCHPHRASE: "I D'wanna."

FAVORITE FOOD: Hamburger

EASINESS TO BEFRIEND: ★★★★★

EVOLUTION: NO EVOLUTIONS
FUSION: NO FUSIONS

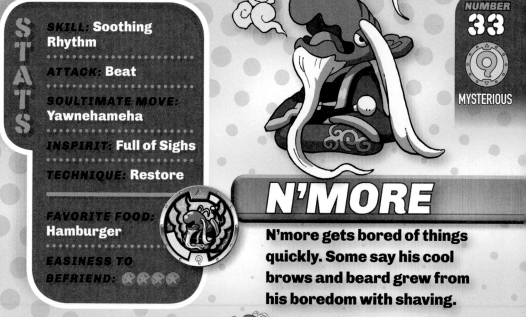

SKILL: Soothing Rhythm

ATTACK: Beat

SOULTIMATE MOVE: Yawnehameha

INSPIRIT: Full of Sighs

TECHNIQUE: Restore

FAVORITE FOOD: Hamburger

EASINESS TO BEFRIEND: ★★★★

N'MORE

N'more gets bored of things quickly. Some say his cool brows and beard grew from his boredom with shaving.

EVOLUTION:

D'wanna level 15 ⇛ N'more

FUSION: NO FUSIONS

RARE!

NUMBER 34

Q'WIT

MYSTERIOUS

RARE! He gives up on everything he tries and won't do the same thing twice. He has a lot of experience at doing things once.

STATS

SKILL: Soothing Rhythm

ATTACK: Beat

SOULTIMATE MOVE: Yawnehameha X

INSPIRIT: Demotivator

TECHNIQUE: Rockslide

FAVORITE FOOD: Hamburger

EASINESS TO BEFRIEND: 

EVOLUTION: NO EVOLUTIONS * **FUSION:** NO FUSIONS

LAFALOTTA

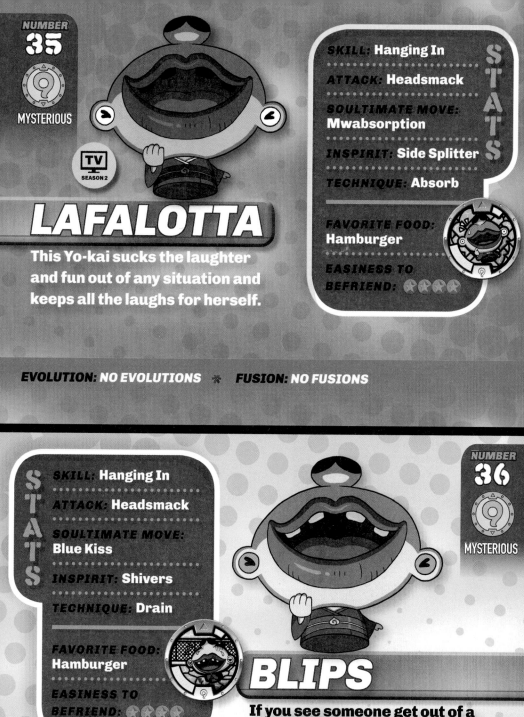

This Yo-kai sucks the laughter and fun out of any situation and keeps all the laughs for herself.

STATS

SKILL: Hanging In

ATTACK: Headsmack

SOULTIMATE MOVE: Mwabsorption

INSPIRIT: Side Splitter

TECHNIQUE: Absorb

FAVORITE FOOD: Hamburger

EASINESS TO BEFRIEND: ★★★★

EVOLUTION: NO EVOLUTIONS * **FUSION:** NO FUSIONS

STATS

SKILL: Hanging In

ATTACK: Headsmack

SOULTIMATE MOVE: Blue Kiss

INSPIRIT: Shivers

TECHNIQUE: Drain

FAVORITE FOOD: Hamburger

EASINESS TO BEFRIEND: ★★★★

BLIPS

If you see someone get out of a pool with blue lips, they might just be inspirited by Blips . . .

EVOLUTION: NO EVOLUTIONS * **FUSION:** NO FUSIONS

NUMBER 37

MYSTERIOUS

TV SEASONS 1 AND 2

TATTLETELL

IN THE VIDEO GAME:

When Tattletell inspirits you, you'll feel inspired to TELL, TELL, TELL all of your secrets.

IN THE ANIMATION:

When Tattletell hung from Katie's chin, the whole school heard about Nate's business.

STATS

SKILL: Caring

ATTACK: Slap

SOULTIMATE MOVE: Loving Slap

INSPIRIT: Disclose

TECHNIQUE: Heal

CATCHPHRASE: "Tell-telllllll!"

FAVORITE FOOD: Ramen

EASINESS TO BEFRIEND: ★★★★

EVOLUTION: NO EVOLUTIONS

FUSION: NO FUSIONS

NUMBER 38

MYSTERIOUS

STATS

SKILL: Caring

ATTACK: Beat

SOULTIMATE MOVE: Max Volume 11!

INSPIRIT: Disclose

TECHNIQUE: Restore

FAVORITE FOOD: Ramen

EASINESS TO BEFRIEND: ★★★

TATTLECAST

She uses her massive speakers to broadcast scandalous secrets to the whole city. Hope they aren't yours!

EVOLUTION: NO EVOLUTIONS

FUSION:

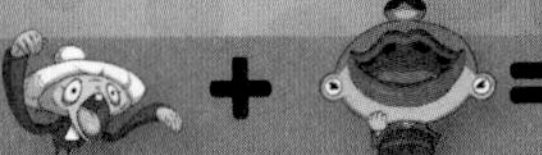

Tattletell + Lafalotta = Tattlecast

NUMBER
39
MYSTERIOUS

SKILL: Caring

ATTACK: Slap

SOULTIMATE MOVE: Skeleton Smack

INSPIRIT: Face Paint

TECHNIQUE: Heal

FAVORITE FOOD: Ramen

EASINESS TO BEFRIEND: ★★★

SKRANNY

Tattletells who discover their love of heavy metal music can don the skull makeup and become a Skranny.

EVOLUTION: NO EVOLUTIONS * **FUSION:** NO FUSIONS

SKILL: Popularity

ATTACK: Shoot

SOULTIMATE MOVE: Kiss of Life

INSPIRIT: Popularize

TECHNIQUE: Whirlwind

FAVORITE FOOD: Bread

EASINESS TO BEFRIEND: ★★★★

NUMBER
40
MYSTERIOUS

CUPISTOL

This debonair Yo-kai is quite a hit with the ladies. Anyone he shoots will love you. He's just the greatest! *swoon*

EVOLUTION: NO EVOLUTIONS * **FUSION:** NO FUSIONS

NUMBER 41

MYSTERIOUS

CASANUVA

This narcissist makes every lady he sees fall in love with him, regardless of age or appearance. Who would want that?!

STATS

SKILL: Popularity

ATTACK: Guns Blazing

SOULTIMATE MOVE: Heavenly Heart

INSPIRIT: Popularize

TECHNIQUE: Storm

FAVORITE FOOD: Bread

EASINESS TO BEFRIEND: ★★★

EVOLUTION: NO EVOLUTIONS ✱ **FUSION:**

Cupistol + Love Buster = Casanuva

STATS

SKILL: Unpopularity

ATTACK: Guns Blazing

SOULTIMATE MOVE: Fiery Longing

INSPIRIT: Unpopularize

TECHNIQUE: Blaze

FAVORITE FOOD: Bread

EASINESS TO BEFRIEND: ★★

NUMBER 42

MYSTERIOUS

CASANONO

Casanuva's opposite. He just can't get a date, no matter what! He'll make you unpopular, too. Best to give him some space.

EVOLUTION: NO EVOLUTIONS ✱ **FUSION:** NO FUSIONS

NUMBER 43

MYSTERIOUS

TV SEASONS 1 AND 2

SIGNIBBLE

IN THE VIDEO GAME:

A mischievous Yo-kai who snacks on radio waves in the air. You'll lose a few bars on your phone when he's around.

IN THE ANIMATION:

When Nate tried to watch TV after bedtime, Signibble had some fun changing the channels. *Zap! Zap!*

STATS

SKILL: Lightning Play

ATTACK: One-Two Punch

SOULTIMATE MOVE: Signal Shock

INSPIRIT: Paralyze

TECHNIQUE: Lightning

CATCHPHRASE: "Zap, zap!"

FAVORITE FOOD: Rice Balls

EASINESS TO BEFRIEND: ★★★★

EVOLUTION: NO EVOLUTIONS

FUSION: NO FUSIONS

NUMBER 44

MYSTERIOUS

SIGNITON

Signiton is almost a deity for those in desperate need of a wireless signal. He can boost your reception if you ask.

STATS

SKILL: Lightning Play

ATTACK: One-Two Punch

SOULTIMATE MOVE: Ton o' Thunder

INSPIRIT: Paralyze

TECHNIQUE: Voltage

FAVORITE FOOD: Rice Balls

EASINESS TO BEFRIEND: ★★★

EVOLUTION: NO EVOLUTIONS ✻ **FUSION:**

 +  = 

Signibble + GHz Orb = Signiton

RARE!

NUMBER
45

MYSTERIOUS

STATIKING

RARE! He's pretty lazy, but if he got motivated, his power would fix a ton of the world's energy problems.

STATS

SKILL: Long Lasting

ATTACK: One-Two Punch

SOULTIMATE MOVE: Giga Turbocharge

INSPIRIT: Electrocute

TECHNIQUE: Voltage

FAVORITE FOOD: Rice Balls

EASINESS TO BEFRIEND: 

EVOLUTION: NO EVOLUTIONS ✱ **FUSION:** NO FUSIONS

MIRAPO

SKILL: Mirror Body

ATTACK: Body Bash

SOULTIMATE MOVE: Mirror to Mirror

INSPIRIT: Mirror Power

TECHNIQUE: Drain

FAVORITE FOOD: Chinese Food

EASINESS TO BEFRIEND: ★★★

IN THE VIDEO GAME:

An ancient mirror that embodied a soul and became a Yo-kai. It can create a portal between two mirrors.

IN THE ANIMATION:

When you wake up in your own bed but don't remember how you got there, thank Mirapo. He got Nate's family back home in a blink of an eye!

EVOLUTION: NO EVOLUTIONS
FUSION: NO FUSIONS

MIRCLE

SKILL: Mirror Body

ATTACK: Body Bash

SOULTIMATE MOVE: Dark World

INSPIRIT: Cursed Mirror

TECHNIQUE: Reaper

FAVORITE FOOD: Chinese Food

EASINESS TO BEFRIEND: ★★★

Mircle fills the space behind mirrors with evil by renting it out to bad Yo-kai . . . at a wickedly high interest rate, naturally.

EVOLUTION: NO EVOLUTIONS * **FUSION:** NO FUSIONS

NUMBER
48

MYSTERIOUS

ILLOO

TV
SEASONS 1 AND 2

IN THE VIDEO GAME:

A caring teacher who uses illusions to simplify his lessons. He can make complex topics seem pretty accessible.

IN THE ANIMATION:

Illoo won third place at the Yo-kai-lympics! His chocobar illusion fooled Jibanyan into chewing on playground equipment.

STATS

SKILL: Brother's Vow

ATTACK: Hit

SOULTIMATE MOVE: Spirit Illusion

INSPIRIT: Illusion Power

TECHNIQUE: Rapids

CATCHPHRASE: "Hoo, hoo, hoo!"

FAVORITE FOOD: Chinese Food

EASINESS TO BEFRIEND: ★★★★

EVOLUTION: NO EVOLUTIONS

FUSION: NO FUSIONS

NUMBER
49

MYSTERIOUS

ELLOO

A friendly old Yo-kai who can dissipate into a haze. He's Illoo's brother.

STATS

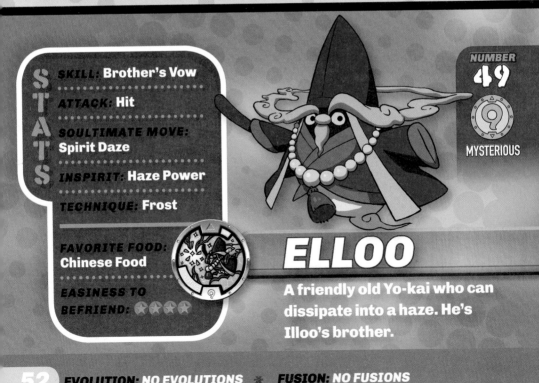

SKILL: Brother's Vow

ATTACK: Hit

SOULTIMATE MOVE: Spirit Daze

INSPIRIT: Haze Power

TECHNIQUE: Frost

FAVORITE FOOD: Chinese Food

EASINESS TO BEFRIEND: ★★★★

EVOLUTION: NO EVOLUTIONS * **FUSION:** NO FUSIONS

NUMBER 50

MYSTERIOUS

ALLOO

He wanders the world without a goal. It's an absolute miracle if the three brothers Illoo, Elloo, and Alloo all meet up.

STATS

SKILL: Brother's Vow

ATTACK: Hit

SOULTIMATE MOVE: Wandering World

INSPIRIT: Wanderlust

TECHNIQUE: Lightning

FAVORITE FOOD: Chinese Food

EASINESS TO BEFRIEND: ★★★

EVOLUTION: NO EVOLUTIONS * **FUSION:** NO FUSIONS

NUMBER 51

MYSTERIOUS

TV SEASON 1

ESPY

STATS

SKILL: Hanging In

ATTACK: Headsmack

SOULTIMATE MOVE: Third Eye

INSPIRIT: Expose Weakness

TECHNIQUE: Rockslide

CATCHPHRASE: "Am I right?"

FAVORITE FOOD: Vegetables

EASINESS TO BEFRIEND: ★★★★

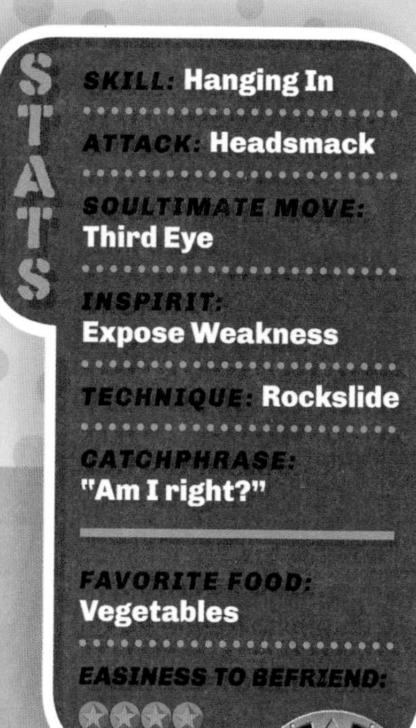

EVOLUTION: NO EVOLUTIONS

FUSION: NO FUSIONS

IN THE VIDEO GAME:

Espy gets a kick out of reading people's minds. It's totally not fair that no one can read hers . . . and now she knows that, too.

IN THE ANIMATION:

When Espy shares Nate's inner thoughts, everyone is embarrassed. So Nate only thinks about the most embarrassing things you can imagine!

NUMBER 52
MYSTERIOUS

TV SEASON 2

INFOUR

Her four eyes can see a person's age, name, and birthday, but she can't read minds. It's still kinda creepy, though.

STATS

SKILL: Hanging In

ATTACK: Headsmack

SOULTIMATE MOVE: Foursight

INSPIRIT: Mysterious Power

TECHNIQUE: Drain

FAVORITE FOOD: Vegetables

EASINESS TO BEFRIEND: ★★★

EVOLUTION: NO EVOLUTIONS
FUSION: NO FUSIONS

NUMBER 53
MYSTERIOUS

TV SEASONS 1 AND 2

TENGU

STATS

SKILL: Wind Play

ATTACK: Nasty Kick

SOULTIMATE MOVE: Typhoon Fan

INSPIRIT: Tengu'd

TECHNIQUE: Storm

FAVORITE FOOD: Candy

EASINESS TO BEFRIEND: —

IN THE VIDEO GAME:

A popular Tengu who controls the power of wind. Apparently all that power comes from his biggest fan.

IN THE ANIMATION:

Whisper swears that the ancient Tengu is his BFF. But when the powerful Yo-kai comes to town, he sends Whisper flying!

EVOLUTION: NO EVOLUTIONS
FUSION: NO FUSIONS

NUMBER 54

FLENGU

MYSTERIOUS

RARE!

RARE! A Tengu with hair the color of fire. Legend says he causes a drought when humanity needs to be taught a lesson.

STATS

SKILL: Fire Play

ATTACK: Nasty Kick

SOULTIMATE MOVE: Blazing Typhoon

INSPIRIT: Burn

TECHNIQUE: Incinerate

FAVORITE FOOD: Candy

EASINESS TO BEFRIEND: 

EVOLUTION: NO EVOLUTIONS * **FUSION:** NO FUSIONS

KYUBI

NUMBER 55

MYSTERIOUS

IN THE VIDEO GAME:

An elite, nine-tailed fox Yo-kai. He can easily produce power greater than a volcanic eruption.

IN THE ANIMATION:

Kyubi believes he is the most beautiful of Yo-kai. His mission is to collect one hundred hearts and get promoted to Senior Fox by the Fox King. But to do this, he must make humans fall in love with him. For his hundredth heart, he chooses Katie!

STATS

SKILL: Sense of Smell

ATTACK: Tail Slap

SOULTIMATE MOVE: Inferno

INSPIRIT: Burn

TECHNIQUE: Incinerate

CATCHPHRASE: "Have you ever seen a Yo-kai as beautiful as *moi*?"

FAVORITE FOOD: Seafood

EASINESS TO BEFRIEND: —

EVOLUTION: NO EVOLUTIONS * **FUSION:** NO FUSIONS

NUMBER 56

MYSTERIOUS

FROSTAIL

RARE!

RARE! Even a single hair of this rare Yo-kai's silvery coat can bring generations of good luck!

STATS

SKILL: Sense of Smell

ATTACK: Tail Slap

SOULTIMATE MOVE: Arctic Abyss

INSPIRIT: Divine Protection

TECHNIQUE: Blizzard

FAVORITE FOOD: Seafood

EASINESS TO BEFRIEND: —

EVOLUTION: *NO EVOLUTIONS* ✱ ***FUSION:*** *NO FUSIONS*

DULLUMA

He looks like a lucky daruma, but his real body is inside the shell. Dull and sluggish, he can really slow you down.

STATS

SKILL: Glossy Skin

ATTACK: Body Bash

SOULTIMATE MOVE: Headbutt HEY-O!

INSPIRIT: Dullness

TECHNIQUE: Pebble

FAVORITE FOOD: Bread

EASINESS TO BEFRIEND: ★★★★★

EVOLUTION: NO EVOLUTIONS ✱ **FUSION:** NO FUSIONS

NUMBER 58

TOUGH

DARUMACHO

Now a truly macho Yo-kai, this one worked tirelessly in a mountain retreat to train away his dullness.

STATS

SKILL: Glossy Skin

ATTACK: Power Punch

SOULTIMATE MOVE: Burning Buster

INSPIRIT: Machismo

TECHNIQUE: Pebble

FAVORITE FOOD: Bread

EASINESS TO BEFRIEND: ★★★

EVOLUTION: NO EVOLUTIONS ✱ **FUSION:**

Dulluma + Mochismo = Darumacho

SKILL: Glossy Skin

ATTACK: Power Punch

SOULTIMATE MOVE: Gorilla Straight

INSPIRIT: Musclehead

TECHNIQUE: Whirlwind

FAVORITE FOOD: Bread

EASINESS TO BEFRIEND: ★★★

GORUMA

Darumacho wasn't happy until he had the body and strength of a gorilla. He can crush cars as easily as marshmallows.

EVOLUTION: NO EVOLUTIONS ✱ **FUSION:** NO FUSIONS

SKILL: Blocker

ATTACK: Body Bash

SOULTIMATE MOVE: No Way Through

INSPIRIT: Refusal

TECHNIQUE: Pebble

CATCHPHRASE: "No way!"

FAVORITE FOOD: Ramen

EASINESS TO BEFRIEND: ★★★★

TV SEASONS 1 AND 2

NOWAY

IN THE VIDEO GAME:

He rejects anything you ask with a terse "No way!" Becoming a brain surgeon astronaut is easier than getting past him.

IN THE ANIMATION:

Noway makes you say "no way" to everything. Nate finally puts a stop to Noway by saying the opposite of what he wants—asking Noway to say, "NOWAY!"

EVOLUTION: NO EVOLUTIONS
FUSION: NO FUSIONS

IMPASS

You . . . you just can't get by Impass. Why?! What's his motivation?! What's the story behind him?! Nobody knows . . .

STATS

SKILL: **Blocker**

ATTACK: **Tackle**

SOULTIMATE MOVE: **Insurmountable**

INSPIRIT: **Refusal**

TECHNIQUE: **Rockslide**

FAVORITE FOOD: **Ramen**

EASINESS TO BEFRIEND: ★★

EVOLUTION:

Noway level 29 ⇛ Impass

FUSION: NO FUSIONS

NUMBER 62

TOUGH

WALLDIN

RARE!

RARE! Formerly a sturdy castle wall, the fall of the family he once protected turned him into a Yo-kai.

STATS

SKILL: Blocker

ATTACK: Tackle

SOULTIMATE MOVE: Stonewall Drop

INSPIRIT: Castle Power

TECHNIQUE: Rockslide

FAVORITE FOOD: Ramen

EASINESS TO BEFRIEND: ★★

EVOLUTION: NO EVOLUTIONS ✱ **FUSION:** NO FUSIONS

NUMBER 63

TOUGH

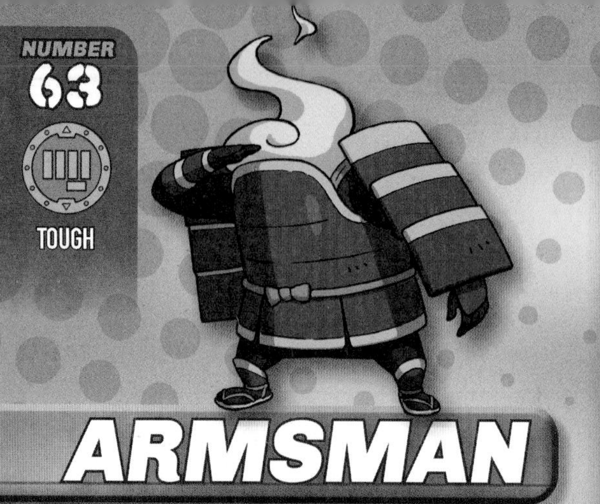

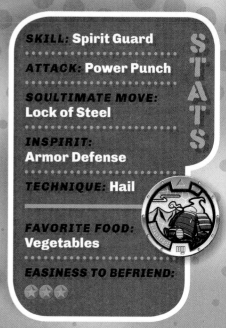

ARMSMAN

He may be headless, but he gives 110 percent. He dreams of reuniting with his head someday . . . Not sure how he dreams, he just does.

STATS

SKILL: Spirit Guard

ATTACK: Power Punch

SOULTIMATE MOVE: Lock of Steel

INSPIRIT: Armor Defense

TECHNIQUE: Hail

FAVORITE FOOD: Vegetables

EASINESS TO BEFRIEND:

EVOLUTION: NO EVOLUTIONS * **FUSION:** NO FUSIONS

STATS

SKILL: Endurance

ATTACK: Fullswing

SOULTIMATE MOVE: Fidgeting Smack

INSPIRIT: Fidgeting

TECHNIQUE: Torrent

CATCHPHRASE: "So much pressure—let it out!"

FAVORITE FOOD: Rice Balls

EASINESS TO BEFRIEND:

EVOLUTION: NO EVOLUTIONS

FUSION: NO FUSIONS

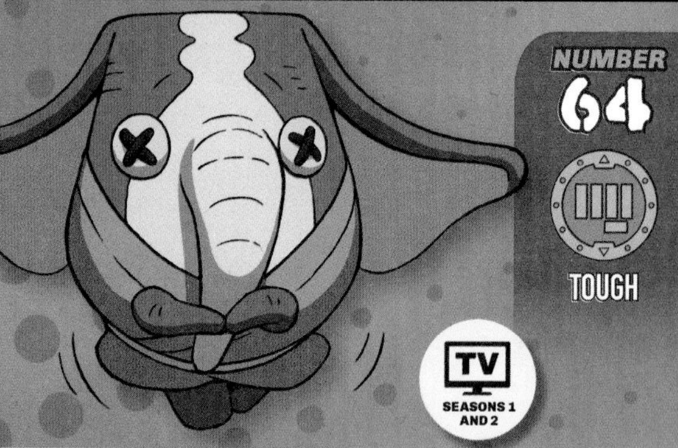

NUMBER 64

TOUGH

TV SEASONS 1 AND 2

FIDGEPHANT

IN THE VIDEO GAME:

Fidgephant always feels like his nose is going to leak. When he has to release it, he attacks with a water stream.

IN THE ANIMATION:

This Yo-kai makes you have to go. And always at the worst possible moment—like during a movie or a test!

NUMBER 65

TOUGH

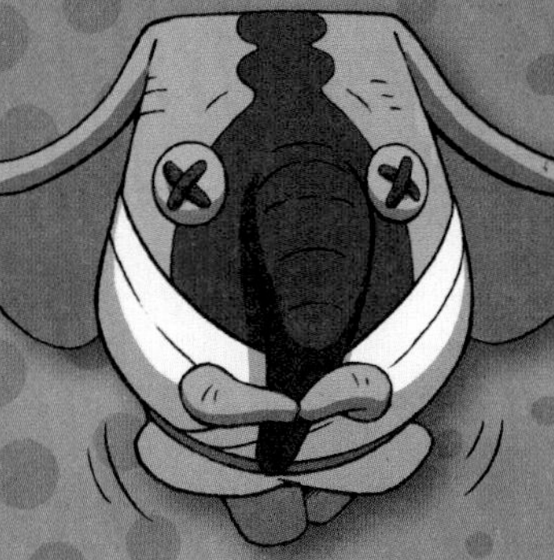

TOUPHANT

Touphant can endure anything . . . with a certain amount of body-shaking effort. He can help you persevere as well.

STATS

SKILL: Endurance

ATTACK: Fullswing

SOULTIMATE MOVE: Trembling Smack

INSPIRIT: Shaking

TECHNIQUE: Rapids

FAVORITE FOOD: Rice Balls

EASINESS TO BEFRIEND: ★★★★

EVOLUTION: NO EVOLUTIONS ✱ **FUSION:** NO FUSIONS

STATS

SKILL: The Stand

ATTACK: Palm Strike

SOULTIMATE MOVE: Barricade Block

INSPIRIT: Needle Poke

TECHNIQUE: Torrent

FAVORITE FOOD: Milk

EASINESS TO BEFRIEND: ★★★★

NUMBER 66

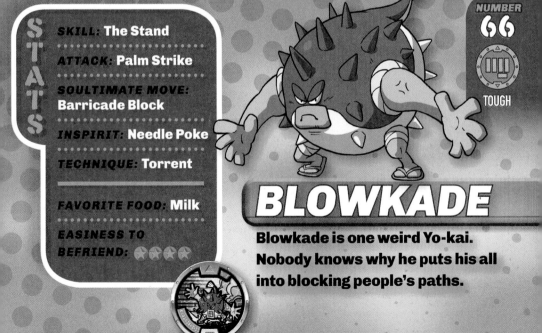

TOUGH

BLOWKADE

Blowkade is one weird Yo-kai. Nobody knows why he puts his all into blocking people's paths.

EVOLUTION: NO EVOLUTIONS ✱ **FUSION:** NO FUSIONS

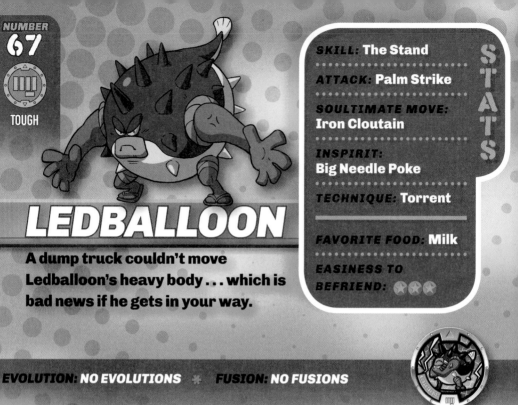

NUMBER 67

TOUGH

LEDBALLOON

A dump truck couldn't move Ledballoon's heavy body . . . which is bad news if he gets in your way.

STATS

SKILL: The Stand

ATTACK: Palm Strike

SOULTIMATE MOVE: Iron Cloutain

INSPIRIT: Big Needle Poke

TECHNIQUE: Torrent

FAVORITE FOOD: Milk

EASINESS TO BEFRIEND: ★★★

EVOLUTION: NO EVOLUTIONS * **FUSION:** NO FUSIONS

NUMBER 68

TOUGH

TV SEASON 2

MAD MOUNTAIN

Hailing from the land of frost, it's the wrestler with legs as thick as glaciers and a heart of ice: MAD MOUNTAIN!

STATS

SKILL: The Stand

ATTACK: Palm Strike

SOULTIMATE MOVE: Ultra Sumo Stomp

INSPIRIT: Perseverance

TECHNIQUE: Hail

FAVORITE FOOD: Rice Balls

EASINESS TO BEFRIEND: ★★★★

EVOLUTION: NO EVOLUTIONS * **FUSION:** NO FUSIONS

LAVA LORD

And in red, we have the only wrestler to rival Mad Mountain, it's the violent volcano himself: LAAAVA LOOOOOOORD!

STATS

SKILL: The Stand

ATTACK: Palm Strike

SOULTIMATE MOVE: Midnight Stomp

INSPIRIT: Volcanic Blessing

TECHNIQUE: Shock

FAVORITE FOOD: Rice Balls

EASINESS TO BEFRIEND: ★★★

EVOLUTION: NO EVOLUTIONS * **FUSION:** NO FUSIONS

ROUGHRAFF

STATS

SKILL: Revenge

ATTACK: Headbutt

SOULTIMATE MOVE: Staredown

INSPIRIT: Rebel Soul

TECHNIQUE: Pebble

CATCHPHRASE: "Hey, Daddy-o!"

FAVORITE FOOD: Ramen

EASINESS TO BEFRIEND: ★★★★

IN THE VIDEO GAME:

A Yo-kai whose only cause is rebellion, he inspirits good kids into being delinquents.

IN THE ANIMATION:

Roughraff is public enemy number one! He's responsible for 98 percent of the troublemakers in the world.

EVOLUTION: NO EVOLUTIONS
FUSION: NO FUSIONS

BADUDE

This gang leader runs into enemy territory wielding his brutal nail bat. That's his way of taking care of his gang.

STATS

SKILL: Revenge

ATTACK: Headbuster

SOULTIMATE MOVE: Gangster Glare

INSPIRIT: Rebel Soul

TECHNIQUE: Pebble

FAVORITE FOOD: Ramen

EASINESS TO BEFRIEND: ★★★

EVOLUTION: 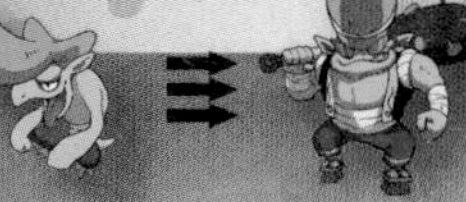

FUSION: NO FUSIONS

Roughraff level 26 ⇛ Badude

BRUFF

RARE!

TV SEASON 2

RARE! Said to have taken down an entire Yo-kai gang by himself. Many rebel Yo-kai revere him as a big brother.

STATS

SKILL: Revenge

ATTACK: Headbuster

SOULTIMATE MOVE: Brutal Butt Bat

INSPIRIT: Enrage

TECHNIQUE: Meteor

FAVORITE FOOD: Ramen

EASINESS TO BEFRIEND:

EVOLUTION: NO EVOLUTIONS * **FUSION:** NO FUSIONS

RHINOGGIN

The hyperaggressive Rhinoggin is always battling Beetler for the title of Bug Yo-kai King.

STATS

SKILL: Guard Break

ATTACK: Fullswing

SOULTIMATE MOVE: Super Horn Crush

INSPIRIT: Rhino Power

TECHNIQUE: Rockslide

FAVORITE FOOD: Vegetables

EASINESS TO BEFRIEND: ★★★

EVOLUTION: NO EVOLUTIONS * **FUSION:** NO FUSIONS

RHINORMOUS

Only the select few Rhinoggins who have proven their might in battle can hold the name of Rhinormous.

STATS

SKILL: Guard Break

ATTACK: Headbuster

SOULTIMATE MOVE: Horn Breaker

INSPIRIT: Peerless Power

TECHNIQUE: Rockslide

FAVORITE FOOD: Vegetables

EASINESS TO BEFRIEND: ★★

EVOLUTION: NO EVOLUTIONS * **FUSION:**

 +  = 

Rhinoggin + Unbeatable Soul = Rhinormous

NUMBER
75

TOUGH

HORNAPLENTY

RARE!

RARE! When Rhinormous achieves power far beyond his peers, he can earn the rarified title of Hornaplenty.

STATS

SKILL: Guard Break

ATTACK: Headbuster

SOULTIMATE MOVE: Horn Explosion

INSPIRIT: Legend Power

TECHNIQUE: Meteor

FAVORITE FOOD: Vegetables

EASINESS TO BEFRIEND: 

EVOLUTION: NO EVOLUTIONS * *FUSION:* NO FUSIONS

NUMBER 76

TOUGH

CASTELIUS III

Castelius III will make you always come in third. There's not much of a future in that . . . unless you're a bronze tycoon.

STATS

SKILL: Bronze Guard

ATTACK: Body Bash

SOULTIMATE MOVE: Self Destruct

INSPIRIT: Bronze Power

TECHNIQUE: Pebble

FAVORITE FOOD: Milk

EASINESS TO BEFRIEND: ★★★

EVOLUTION: NO EVOLUTIONS ✱ **FUSION:** NO FUSIONS

STATS

SKILL: Silver Guard

ATTACK: Tackle

SOULTIMATE MOVE: Refined Guard

INSPIRIT: Silver Power

TECHNIQUE: Frost

FAVORITE FOOD: Milk

EASINESS TO BEFRIEND: ★★★

NUMBER 77

TOUGH

CASTELIUS II

Castelius II will always lock you in second place. Not bad, but could you have done a bit better . . . ?

EVOLUTION: NO EVOLUTIONS ✱ **FUSION:**  +  = 

Castelius III + Castelius III = Castelius II

CASTELIUS I

First place. Gold medals. Big trophies. That's your life if Castelius I inspirits you. But with great power comes great . . . ness!

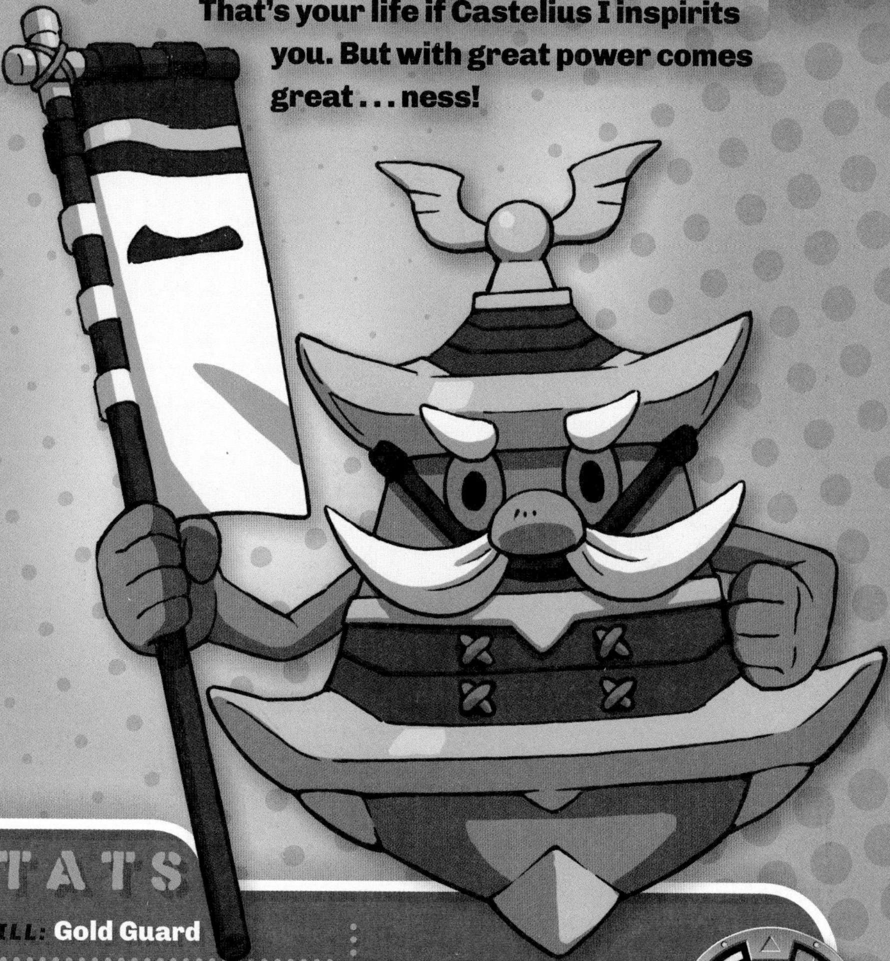

STATS

SKILL: Gold Guard

ATTACK: Bone Crusher

SOULTIMATE MOVE: Glorious Buh-bye

INSPIRIT: Gold Power

TECHNIQUE: Lightning

FAVORITE FOOD: Milk

EASINESS TO BEFRIEND: ★★

EVOLUTION: NO EVOLUTIONS

FUSION:  +  = 

Castelius II + Castelius II = Castelius I

RARE!

NUMBER 79

CASTELIUS MAX

TOUGH

RARE! Being inspirited by this extremely rare Yo-kai will let you transcend mere winning and losing.

STATS

SKILL: Platinum Gold

ATTACK: Bone Crusher

SOULTIMATE MOVE: Luxury Platinum Guard

INSPIRIT: Platinum Power

TECHNIQUE: Tornado

FAVORITE FOOD: Milk

EASINESS TO BEFRIEND: 

EVOLUTION: NO EVOLUTIONS * **FUSION:**  +  =  

Castelius I + Platinum Bar = Castelius Max

NUMBER 80

TOUGH

ROBONYAN

RARE!

IN THE VIDEO GAME:

RARE! A robot that thinks it's actually Jibanyan. Stiff movement aside, the resemblance is uncatty! Meow meow.

IN THE ANIMATION:

Robonyan hails from the future and has his very own chocobar factory in his stomach! The only problem is it takes a country's worth of energy to recharge his batteries.

STATS

SKILL: Blocker

ATTACK: Rocket punch

SOULTIMATE MOVE: Guard Meowde

INSPIRIT: Steel Power

TECHNIQUE: Frost

CATCHPHRASE: "I'll be back."

FAVORITE FOOD: Seafood

EASINESS TO BEFRIEND: ★★

EVOLUTION: NO EVOLUTIONS ✱ **FUSION:** NO FUSIONS

NUMBER 81

TOUGH

GOLDENYAN

RARE!

TV SEASON 2

RARE!

Goldenyan glistens with purrfection. Meow meow. Truly priceless.

STATS

SKILL: Gold Guard

ATTACK: Rocket Punch

SOULTIMATE MOVE: Gold Thundpurr

INSPIRIT: Golden Power

TECHNIQUE: Shock

FAVORITE FOOD: Seafood

EASINESS TO BEFRIEND: —

EVOLUTION: NO EVOLUTIONS * **FUSION:** NO FUSIONS

DROMP

TOUGH

Fairy tales tell of the monstrous Dromp building mountains and digging ponds.

STATS

SKILL: Insulator

ATTACK: Steamroll

SOULTIMATE MOVE: Total Collapse

INSPIRIT: Earth Healing

TECHNIQUE: Pebble

FAVORITE FOOD: Vegetables

EASINESS TO BEFRIEND: —

EVOLUTION: NO EVOLUTIONS * **FUSION:** NO FUSIONS

RARE!

NUMBER 83

SWOSH

RARE! A Yo-kai with a heart as big as the ocean. Some say that Swosh embodies the sea itself.

STATS

SKILL: Blessed Body

ATTACK: Steamroll

SOULTIMATE MOVE: Tidal Guard

INSPIRIT: Ocean Power

TECHNIQUE: Torrent

FAVORITE FOOD: Vegetables

EASINESS TO BEFRIEND: 

EVOLUTION: NO EVOLUTIONS * **FUSION:** NO FUSIONS

NUMBER 84

CHARMING

DAZZABEL

IN THE VIDEO GAME:

Dazzabel loves wearing anything gaudy. If she inspirits you, you'll start liking that style, too!

IN THE ANIMATION:

Dazzabel inspirited Nate's mom at the worst possible time—Parent Day at school!

STATS

SKILL: Hanging In

ATTACK: Pesky Poke

SOULTIMATE MOVE: ★ Stylish Stab

INSPIRIT: Makeover

TECHNIQUE: Fire

CATCHPHRASE: "Faaaaaancy!"

FAVORITE FOOD: Hamburger

EASINESS TO BEFRIEND: ★★★★

EVOLUTION: NO EVOLUTIONS * **FUSION:** NO FUSIONS

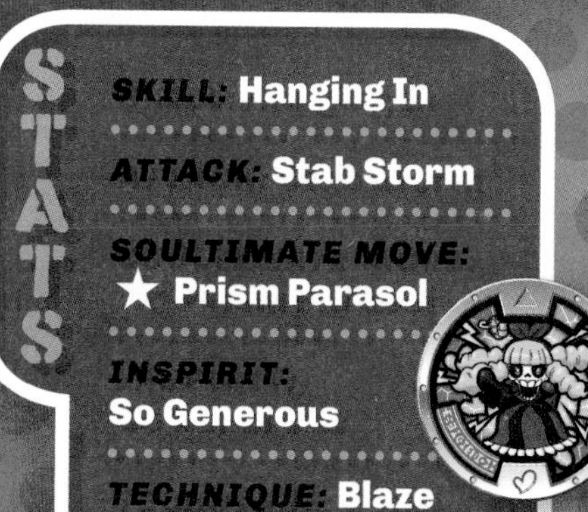

STATS

SKILL: Hanging In

ATTACK: Stab Storm

SOULTIMATE MOVE: ★ Prism Parasol

INSPIRIT: So Generous

TECHNIQUE: Blaze

FAVORITE FOOD: Hamburger

EASINESS TO BEFRIEND: ★★★

NUMBER 85

CHARMING

RATTELLE

While she looks calm in her gothic wear, she'll fly into a rage if you insult her style.

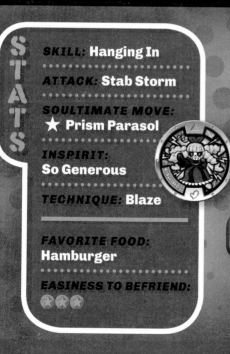

EVOLUTION: NO EVOLUTIONS * **FUSION:**

Dazzabel + Cupistol = Rattelle

RARE!

NUMBER
86

SKELEBELLA

RARE! She's so confident in the unparalleled beauty of her bones that she doesn't even need her skin.

STATS

SKILL: Hanging In

ATTACK: Pointy Pokes

SOULTIMATE MOVE: ★ Radiant Rain

INSPIRIT: So Generous

TECHNIQUE: Rapids

FAVORITE FOOD: Hamburger

EASINESS TO BEFRIEND: 

EVOLUTION: NO EVOLUTIONS ✱ **FUSION:** NO FUSIONS

NUMBER 87

CHARMING

CADIN

TV SEASON 1

IN THE VIDEO GAME:

He claims to practice "cicada ninjutsu" . . . but that's not really a thing. Unless it's a mastery of running away.

IN THE ANIMATION:

As a cicada, Cadin only lived one week. As a Yo-kai, he believed he only had one week to live unless he stayed underground.

STATS

SKILL: Modest

ATTACK: Stepping Slice

SOULTIMATE MOVE: Cicada Cut

INSPIRIT: Cicada Ninjutsu

TECHNIQUE: Whirlwind

CATCHPHRASE: "Ming Ming!"

FAVORITE FOOD: Juice

EASINESS TO BEFRIEND: ★★★★

EVOLUTION: *NO EVOLUTIONS*

FUSION: *NO FUSIONS*

NUMBER 88

CHARMING

CADABLE

Cadin has trained his "cicada ninjutsu" to its peak. Now Cadable claims that it's a worthy martial art! *crickets* *cicadas*

STATS

SKILL: Modest

ATTACK: Double Slice

SOULTIMATE MOVE: Shadow Speed

INSPIRIT: Cicada Ninjutsu

TECHNIQUE: Tornado

FAVORITE FOOD: Juice

EASINESS TO BEFRIEND: ★★★

EVOLUTION:

Cadin level 21 ⇶ Cadable

FUSION: *NO FUSIONS*

RARE!

NUMBER
89

CHARMING

SINGCADA

RARE! His advanced style of "cicada ninjutsu" makes him sing while he fights! His battles even draw music fans sometimes!

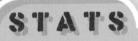

SKILL: Eye Sight A

ATTACK: Double Slice

SOULTIMATE MOVE: Wind Run

INSPIRIT: Radical Ninjutsu

TECHNIQUE: Blaze

FAVORITE FOOD: Juice

EASINESS TO BEFRIEND: ★★★

EVOLUTION: NO EVOLUTIONS ✱ **FUSION:** NO FUSIONS

NUMBER 90

CHARMING

PUPSICLE

Pupsicle is always cold. He may be inspiriting those who wear layers of clothes in summer.

STATS

SKILL: Penetrate

ATTACK: Bite

SOULTIMATE MOVE: Icicle Crack

INSPIRIT: Chills

TECHNIQUE: Frost

FAVORITE FOOD: Ramen

EASINESS TO BEFRIEND: ★★★★

EVOLUTION: NO EVOLUTIONS * **FUSION:** NO FUSIONS

NUMBER 91

CHARMING

CHILHUAHUA

Legends tell of Chilhuahua saving people lost in the snowy mountains. Some consider him a deity.

STATS

SKILL: Penetrate

ATTACK: Ventilator

SOULTIMATE MOVE: Sub-Zero

INSPIRIT: Freeze

TECHNIQUE: Blizzard

FAVORITE FOOD: Ramen

EASINESS TO BEFRIEND: ★★

EVOLUTION: NO EVOLUTIONS * **FUSION:**  +  =  

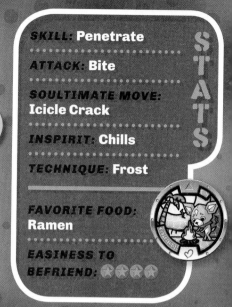

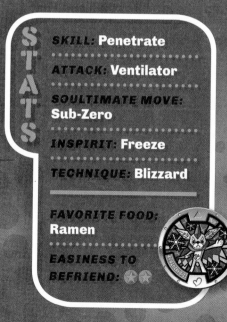

Pupsicle + Snowstorm Cloak = Chilhuahua

RARE!

SWELTERRIER

RARE! He always feels like he's too hot due to his fiery heart and body. Being near him is like being near a space heater.

STATS

SKILL: Fire Watchout

ATTACK: Ventilator

SOULTIMATE MOVE: Heat Wave

INSPIRIT: Blazing Heart

TECHNIQUE: Incinerate

FAVORITE FOOD: Ramen

EASINESS TO BEFRIEND: ★★

EVOLUTION: NO EVOLUTIONS * **FUSION:** NO FUSIONS

NUMBER
93

TV SEASONS 1 AND 2

JIBANYAN

CHARMING

IN THE VIDEO GAME:

After being run over by a car, he inspirits an intersection and seeks to get his revenge on passing cars.

IN THE ANIMATION:

Nate is really impressed with this chocobar-loving Yo-kai's devotion to proving he's not just a lame cat. Nate offers Jibanyan what he really wants—a home—and the two become best friends.

STATS

SKILL: Adrenaline

ATTACK: Sharp Claws

SOULTIMATE MOVE: Paws of Fury

INSPIRIT: Slow Down

TECHNIQUE: Fire

CAT-PHRASES: "I am a cat and I like it like that!"

FAVORITE FOOD: Seafood and chocobars

EASINESS TO BEFRIEND: 

EVOLUTION: ***NO EVOLUTIONS*** ***FUSION:*** ***NO FUSIONS***

NUMBER 94

THORNYAN

CHARMING

TV SEASON 2

IN THE VIDEO GAME:

Jibanyan's proud of his new spiky body. Just don't walk behind him while you're barefoot.

IN THE ANIMATION:

When Jibanyan gets a cold, he becomes Thornyan. Watch out for when he sneezes!

STATS

SKILL: Spiky Guard

ATTACK: Ventilator

SOULTIMATE MOVE: Thorny Thwacks

INSPIRIT: Needle Poke

TECHNIQUE: Tornado

CAT-PHRASE: "Nya-choo!"

FAVORITE FOOD: Seafood

EASINESS TO BEFRIEND: ★★★

EVOLUTION: NO EVOLUTIONS

FUSION:

 +  = 

Jibanyan + Coughkoff = Thornyan

BADDINYAN

CHARMING

IN THE VIDEO GAME:

Jibanyan gone bad. REAL BAD. With an impressive ducktail haircut and classy tails, he's a delinquent without a cause.

IN THE ANIMATION:

When Roughraff inspirited Jibanyan, Jibanyan turned into the no-good Baddinyan. This rebel version of Jibanyan doesn't care about his bad reputation. He just lives for today—chocobar-stained paws and all.

STATS

SKILL: Pompadour

ATTACK: Nasty Kick

SOULTIMATE MOVE: Nyice ta Beatcha

INSPIRIT: Delinquency

TECHNIQUE: Fire

CAT-PHRASE: "It's good to be bad."

FAVORITE FOOD: Seafood

EASINESS TO BEFRIEND: ★★

EVOLUTION: NO EVOLUTIONS

FUSION:

 +  = 

Jibanyan + Roughraff = Baddinyan

WALKAPPA

IN THE VIDEO GAME:

Most kappas stay in the water, but this one likes to walk around. He pours water on his head to make up for this.

IN THE ANIMATION:

This weird-looking duck-dude wears a plate on his head. Walkappa is one chilled-out Yo-kai. He wants everyone to just chill.

STATS

SKILL: Skilled Loafer

ATTACK: Punch

SOULTIMATE MOVE: Mega Waterfall

INSPIRIT: Nap Time

TECHNIQUE: Rapids

CATCHPHRASE: "Totally bogus, man."

FAVORITE FOOD: Vegetables and pizza

EASINESS TO BEFRIEND: ★★★

EVOLUTION: NO EVOLUTIONS

FUSION: NO FUSIONS

APPAK

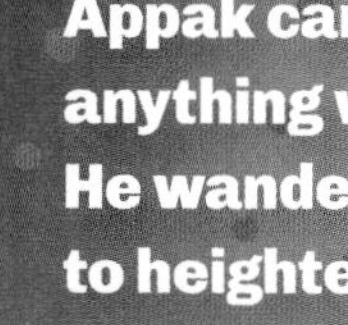

Appak can cut just about anything with his water sword. He wanders the world in order to heighten his skills.

STATS

SKILL: Penetrate

ATTACK: Double Slice

SOULTIMATE MOVE: Torrent Slash

INSPIRIT: Torrent Power

TECHNIQUE: Waterfall

FAVORITE FOOD: Vegetables

EASINESS TO BEFRIEND: ★★★

EVOLUTION:   

Walkappa level 32 ⇛ *Appak*

FUSION: NO FUSIONS

RARE!

NUMBER 98

CHARMING

SUPYO

RARE! Whereas most kappas stick to rivers, this one likes to surf . . . and pick up girls while he's at it.

STATS

SKILL: Penetrate

ATTACK: Double Slice

SOULTIMATE MOVE: Bodacious Slash

INSPIRIT: Surf Power

TECHNIQUE: Waterfall

FAVORITE FOOD: Vegetables

EASINESS TO BEFRIEND: 

EVOLUTION: NO EVOLUTIONS * **FUSION:** NO FUSIONS

KOMASAN

CHARMING

IN THE VIDEO GAME:

Komasan is a guardian lion-dog that got bored of guarding his shrine. Now he's looking for a new one.

IN THE ANIMATION:

When it comes to ice cream, this country bumpkin can't rightly control himself. When he eats ice cream, he's happier than a newborn lamb in spring!

STATS

SKILL: Alpha

ATTACK: Punch

SOULTIMATE MOVE: Spirit Dance

INSPIRIT: Burn

TECHNIQUE: Blaze

CATCHPHRASE: "Oh my swirls!"

FAVORITE FOOD: Milk

EASINESS TO BEFRIEND: ★★★

EVOLUTION: NO EVOLUTIONS

FUSION: NO FUSIONS

KOMANE

Komasan's travels made him grow up into a brave and dependable Yo-kai. He's strong, too!

STATS

SKILL: Alpha

ATTACK: Power Punch

SOULTIMATE MOVE: Spirit Burst

INSPIRIT: Burn

TECHNIQUE: Incinerate

FAVORITE FOOD: Milk

EASINESS TO BEFRIEND: ★★

EVOLUTION:

Komasan level 35 ⇛ Komane

FUSION: *NO FUSIONS*

KOMAJIRO

STATS

SKILL: Omega

ATTACK: Punch

SOULTIMATE MOVE: Wild Zaps

INSPIRIT: Tiger Power

TECHNIQUE: Lightning

CATCHPHRASE: "Hey, big brother!"

FAVORITE FOOD: Milk

EASINESS TO BEFRIEND: ★★★★

EVOLUTION: *NO EVOLUTIONS*
FUSION: *NO FUSIONS*

IN THE VIDEO GAME:

Komasan's younger twin, he looks for his runaway bro. But he can't find him anywhere, poor guy.

IN THE ANIMATION:

Komajiro searched high and low and far and wide for his big brother, Komasan. Once he found him, everything was just right as rain.

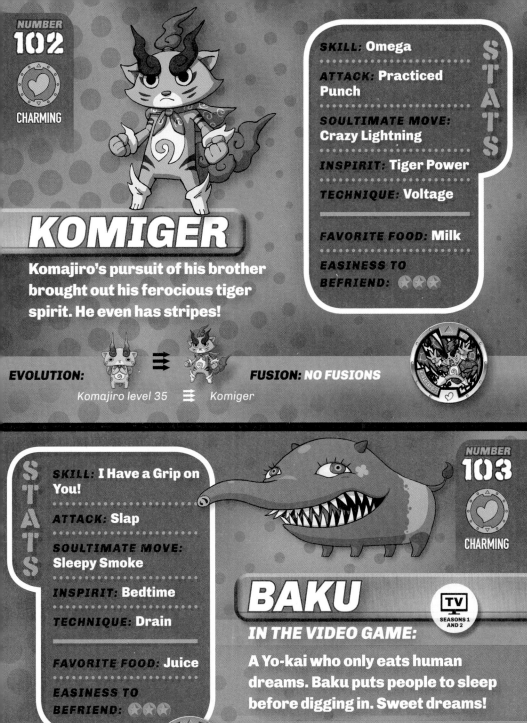

KOMIGER

Komajiro's pursuit of his brother brought out his ferocious tiger spirit. He even has stripes!

STATS

SKILL: Omega

ATTACK: Practiced Punch

SOULTIMATE MOVE: Crazy Lightning

INSPIRIT: Tiger Power

TECHNIQUE: Voltage

FAVORITE FOOD: Milk

EASINESS TO BEFRIEND: ★★★

EVOLUTION:  

Komajiro level 35 ⇛ Komiger

FUSION: ***NO FUSIONS***

NUMBER 103

CHARMING

BAKU

TV SEASONS 1 AND 2

IN THE VIDEO GAME:

A Yo-kai who only eats human dreams. Baku puts people to sleep before digging in. Sweet dreams!

IN THE ANIMATION:

Baku is responsible for the "I just had an awesome dream but I can't remember any of it" phenomenon.

STATS

SKILL: I Have a Grip on You!

ATTACK: Slap

SOULTIMATE MOVE: Sleepy Smoke

INSPIRIT: Bedtime

TECHNIQUE: Drain

FAVORITE FOOD: Juice

EASINESS TO BEFRIEND: ★★★

EVOLUTION: ***NO EVOLUTIONS***

FUSION: ***NO FUSIONS***

RARE!

NUMBER
104

WHAPIR

CHARMING

RARE! A rare white Baku. Legends say that if a Whapir inspirits you, you're guaranteed to have good dreams.

STATS

SKILL: Good Fortune

ATTACK: Slap

SOULTIMATE MOVE: Daydream

INSPIRIT: Sweet Dreams

TECHNIQUE: Drain

FAVORITE FOOD: Juice

EASINESS TO BEFRIEND: 

EVOLUTION: NO EVOLUTIONS * **FUSION:** NO FUSIONS

NUMBER 105

CHARMING

SHMOOPIE

This Yo-kai is cute enough to melt anyone's heart . . . and he knows it! He can be quite the schemer, so look out!

STATS

SKILL: Popularity

ATTACK: Bite

SOULTIMATE MOVE: Heartstring Tug

INSPIRIT: Skip a Beat

TECHNIQUE: Restore

CATCHPHRASE: "Forgive me like donuts!"

FAVORITE FOOD: Hamburger

EASINESS TO BEFRIEND:

EVOLUTION: NO EVOLUTIONS * **FUSION:** NO FUSIONS

NUMBER 106

CHARMING

STATS

SKILL: Popularity

ATTACK: Beat

SOULTIMATE MOVE: Heartmelt Love

INSPIRIT: Skip a Beat

TECHNIQUE: Paradise

FAVORITE FOOD: Hamburger

EASINESS TO BEFRIEND:

PINKIPOO

Known as the Aristocrat of Love, Pinkipoo uses his overpowering cuteness to win over new followers.

EVOLUTION: NO EVOLUTIONS * **FUSION:**

 +  = 

Shmoopie + Love Scepter = Pinkipoo

NUMBER
107

CHARMING

POOKIVIL

RARE! This Yo-kai will make even nice people into scheming manipulators. An embodiment of Pinkipoo's bad side.

STATS

SKILL: Unpopularity

ATTACK: Beat

SOULTIMATE MOVE: Twisted Love

INSPIRIT: Trickery

TECHNIQUE: Reaper

FAVORITE FOOD: Hamburger

EASINESS TO BEFRIEND: ★★

EVOLUTION: NO EVOLUTIONS * **FUSION:** NO FUSIONS

FROSTINA

Frostina has the power to freeze anything, but that keeps her pretty chilly . . . that and bad circulation.

STATS

SKILL: Snow Play

ATTACK: Slap

SOULTIMATE MOVE: Snow Sherbet

INSPIRIT: Numbify

TECHNIQUE: Blizzard

FAVORITE FOOD: Candy

EASINESS TO BEFRIEND: ★★★

EVOLUTION: NO EVOLUTIONS * **FUSION:** NO FUSIONS

BLIZZARIA

Now she can fully control her chilling power. Blizzaria can make snow fall in summer and freeze volcanoes.

STATS

SKILL: Snow Play

ATTACK: Smack Down

SOULTIMATE MOVE: Shiny Snowdrifts

INSPIRIT: Numbify

TECHNIQUE: Blizzard

FAVORITE FOOD: Candy

EASINESS TO BEFRIEND: —

EVOLUTION: NO EVOLUTIONS * **FUSION:**

 +  = 

Frostina + Glacial Clip = Blizzaria

DAMONA

CHARMING

RARE! The princess of a small netherworld region. Her power is immense, but she lacks the power to feel any emotion.

SKILL: Cursed Skin

ATTACK: Smack Down

SOULTIMATE MOVE:
★ Shiny Chaos

INSPIRIT: Curse of Darkness

TECHNIQUE: Blizzard

FAVORITE FOOD: Candy

EASINESS TO BEFRIEND: —

EVOLUTION: NO EVOLUTIONS ✻ **FUSION:** NO FUSIONS

NUMBER 111

HEARTFUL

TV SEASONS 1 AND 2

WIGLIN

SKILL: Wavy Body

ATTACK: Slap

SOULTIMATE MOVE: Wiggling Wave

INSPIRIT: Healthy Wakame

TECHNIQUE: Heal

CATCHPHRASE: "Woo!"

FAVORITE FOOD: Ramen

EASINESS TO BEFRIEND: ★★★★

IN THE VIDEO GAME:

A seaweed Yo-kai who wants to spread his hometown dance to the world. And he's very healthy, too!

IN THE ANIMATION:

This wiggly piece of seaweed is part of the Yo-kai Dance Trio.

EVOLUTION: NO EVOLUTIONS

FUSION: NO FUSIONS

NUMBER 112

HEARTFUL

TV SEASONS 1 AND 2

STEPPA

SKILL: Wavy Body

ATTACK: Slap

SOULTIMATE MOVE: Mambo Madness

INSPIRIT: Kombu Energy

TECHNIQUE: Heal

CATCHPHRASE: "Uh huh, uh huh!"

FAVORITE FOOD: Ramen

EASINESS TO BEFRIEND: ★★★★★

IN THE VIDEO GAME:

Steppa is one of Wiglin's rivals. He believes that kombu is the best kind of seaweed . . . if there is such a thing.

IN THE ANIMATION:

Steppa is a movin' and groovin' member of the Yo-kai Dance Trio.

EVOLUTION: NO EVOLUTIONS

FUSION: NO FUSIONS

NUMBER 113

HEARTFUL

RHYTH

SKILL: Wavy Body

ATTACK: Slap

SOULTIMATE MOVE: Seaweed Samba

INSPIRIT: Slippery Mekabu

TECHNIQUE: Restore

CATCHPHRASE: "All right, all right!"

FAVORITE FOOD: Ramen

EASINESS TO BEFRIEND: ★★★

IN THE VIDEO GAME:

The one female of the seaweed trio. Wiglin and Steppa both really like her, but she doesn't seem to notice.

IN THE ANIMATION:

As a member of the Yo-kai Dance Trio, Rhyth believes you can dance anytime and anyplace. Nate learned that the hard way—and he does not agree.

EVOLUTION: NO EVOLUTIONS
FUSION: NO FUSIONS

NUMBER 114

HEARTFUL

WANTSTON

SKILL: Greed

ATTACK: Slap

SOULTIMATE MOVE: Envious Hand

INSPIRIT: Envy

TECHNIQUE: Shock

FAVORITE FOOD: Ramen

EASINESS TO BEFRIEND: ★★★★★

Wantston wants everything others have, but won't even try to acquire what he envies. So, no worries.

EVOLUTION: NO EVOLUTIONS ✱ **FUSION:** NO FUSIONS

NUMBER 115

GRUBSNITCH

HEARTFUL

IN THE VIDEO GAME:

If you can't stop snacking before dinner, Grubsnitch is probably nearby.

TV SEASONS 1 AND 2

IN THE ANIMATION:

Grubsnitch is famous in pastry circles. Before him, doughnuts didn't have holes. They called them "danishes." He convinced Nate's mom that sampling, snacking, and snitching is much more fun than having a real meal.

STATS

SKILL: Snitch

ATTACK: Smack Down

SOULTIMATE MOVE: Grub Stealer

INSPIRIT: Gluttony

TECHNIQUE: Rockslide

CATCHPHRASE: "It's just a little bite . . .!"

FAVORITE FOOD: Ramen

EASINESS TO BEFRIEND: ★★★★

EVOLUTION: NO EVOLUTIONS ✱ **FUSION:** NO FUSIONS

NUMBER 116

HEARTFUL

TV SEASONS 1 AND 2

HUNGRAMPS

IN THE VIDEO GAME:

A Yo-kai who is always hungry and can make other tummies rumble . . . That's really about the only thing he can do.

IN THE ANIMATION:

This sweet, gentle Yo-kai was once a grandpa. Now he lurks around a convenience store hoping to spot his long-lost granddaughter . . .

STATS

SKILL: Starver

ATTACK: Headsmack

SOULTIMATE MOVE: Hungry Impact

INSPIRIT: Starve

TECHNIQUE: Heal

CATCHPHRASE: "Hungryyyy!"

FAVORITE FOOD: Rice Balls

EASINESS TO BEFRIEND: ★★★★★

EVOLUTION: NO EVOLUTIONS

FUSION: NO FUSIONS

NUMBER 117

HEARTFUL

HUNGORGE

A terribly gluttonous Yo-kai who will eat anything in front of him. His mouth is like a black hole . . . even rice can't escape it.

STATS

SKILL: Starver

ATTACK: Bite

SOULTIMATE MOVE: Gleeful Gluttony

INSPIRIT: Starve

TECHNIQUE: Absorb

FAVORITE FOOD: Rice Balls

EASINESS TO BEFRIEND: ★★★

EVOLUTION:

Hungramps level 22 ⇛ Hungorge

FUSION: NO FUSIONS

NUMBER
118

HEARTFUL

GRAINPA

RARE!

RARE! A Hungramps with a body made of rice. He's so kind, he'll let a hungry person eat part of his body if necessary.

STATS

SKILL: Blessed Body

ATTACK: Headsmack

SOULTIMATE MOVE: Fresh Impact

INSPIRIT: Rice's Kindness

TECHNIQUE: Heal

FAVORITE FOOD: Rice Balls

EASINESS TO BEFRIEND: 

EVOLUTION: NO EVOLUTIONS ✱ **FUSION:** NO FUSIONS

NUMBER
119

HEARTFUL

LODO

You know when you just keep losing change or getting the wrong change back? Lodo's fault.

STATS

SKILL: Stealing

ATTACK: Kick

SOULTIMATE MOVE: I Want It All!

INSPIRIT: Poverty

TECHNIQUE: Whirlwind

FAVORITE FOOD: Milk

EASINESS TO BEFRIEND: ★★★★★

EVOLUTION: NO EVOLUTIONS * **FUSION:** NO FUSIONS

STATS

SKILL: Optimum Power

ATTACK: Flip Kick

SOULTIMATE MOVE: Carefree Hero

INSPIRIT: Optimism

TECHNIQUE: Torrent

FAVORITE FOOD: Milk

EASINESS TO BEFRIEND: ★★★★

NUMBER
120

HEARTFUL

CHIPPA

An eternal optimist who never worries about anything. Being inspirited by him can be worse than you think.

EVOLUTION: NO EVOLUTIONS * **FUSION:** NO FUSIONS

NUMBER 121

HEARTFUL

ENERFLY

TV SEASON 2

A butterfly Yo-kai who brings anyone it inspirits to their peak condition. Often mistaken for Enefly.

SKILL: Miraculous Scales

ATTACK: Slap

SOULTIMATE MOVE: Energy Heaven

INSPIRIT: Energize

TECHNIQUE: Heal

FAVORITE FOOD: Juice

EASINESS TO BEFRIEND: ★★★★

EVOLUTION: NO EVOLUTIONS * **FUSION:** NO FUSIONS

NUMBER 122

HEARTFUL

SKILL: Miraculous Scales

ATTACK: Slap

SOULTIMATE MOVE: Enemy Aura

INSPIRIT: Enemy Maker

TECHNIQUE: Absorb

FAVORITE FOOD: Juice

EASINESS TO BEFRIEND: ★★★★

ENEFLY

A butterfly Yo-kai who makes anyone it inspirits cut ties with their best friend. Often mistaken for Enerfly.

EVOLUTION: NO EVOLUTIONS * **FUSION:** NO FUSIONS

NUMBER 123

HEARTFUL

BETTERFLY

People will fulfill their potential in ways they've never imagined with Betterfly. Everyone wants this Yo-kai!

STATS

SKILL: Miraculous Scales

ATTACK: Smack Down

SOULTIMATE MOVE: Bestacular

INSPIRIT: Feeling Fine

TECHNIQUE: Paradise

FAVORITE FOOD: Juice

EASINESS TO BEFRIEND: ★★

EVOLUTION: NO EVOLUTIONS ✱ **FUSION:**

 +  = 

Enefly + Enerfly = Betterfly

NUMBER 124

HEARTFUL

PEPPILLON

RARE!

IN THE VIDEO GAME:

RARE! A butterfly Yo-kai with otherworldly wings. Breathing in his scales will boost your level of excitement to his max.

IN THE ANIMATION:

Peppillon is responsible for making parents drag their children to boring places like museums and history reenactments. He made Nate's family's spring break seem epic . . . until Drizzle showed up.

STATS

SKILL: Miraculous Scales

ATTACK: Smack Down

SOULTIMATE MOVE: Party Miracle

INSPIRIT: Life Is Good

TECHNIQUE: Paradise

FAVORITE FOOD: Juice

EASINESS TO BEFRIEND: ★★

EVOLUTION: NO EVOLUTIONS * **FUSION:** NO FUSIONS

NUMBER 125

HEARTFUL

TV SEASONS 1 AND 2

HAPPIERRE

IN THE VIDEO GAME:
This heartwarming Yo-kai removes the tension in the air. He can cheer up even the angriest of people.

IN THE ANIMATION:
Happierre makes everything bright and happy. He's married to Dismarelda, who makes everything dark and dreary. Together, they create normalcy.

STATS

SKILL: Caring

ATTACK: Body Bash

SOULTIMATE MOVE: Air of Happiness

INSPIRIT: Cheerfulness

TECHNIQUE: Restore

CATCHPHRASE: "Hon hon hon hon!"

FAVORITE FOOD: Bread

EASINESS TO BEFRIEND: ★★★★

EVOLUTION: NO EVOLUTIONS
FUSION: NO FUSIONS

NUMBER 126

HEARTFUL

REVERSA

STATS

SKILL: Insecure

ATTACK: Tackle

SOULTIMATE MOVE: Fun Field

INSPIRIT: Insecurity

TECHNIQUE: Paradise

FAVORITE FOOD: Bread

EASINESS TO BEFRIEND: ★★★

One moment she's happy, and the next, she's sad. She can be more difficult to deal with than Dismarelda sometimes.

EVOLUTION: NO EVOLUTIONS * **FUSION:**

 +  =  

Happierre + Dismarelda = Reversa

NUMBER
127

HEARTFUL

REVERSETTE

RARE!

RARE! She resembles Reversa, but her reversed pattern is a rare sight. Her depression . . . not so rare.

STATS

SKILL: Insecure

ATTACK: Tackle

SOULTIMATE MOVE: Zany Zone

INSPIRIT: Insecurity

TECHNIQUE: Storm

FAVORITE FOOD: Bread

EASINESS TO BEFRIEND: ★★

EVOLUTION: NO EVOLUTIONS ✱ **FUSION:** NO FUSIONS

HEARTFUL

OL' SAINT TRICK

Take a guess and get one of three presents: bad, good, or average. He'll leave if you ask for all three, though . . .

TV SEASON 2

STATS

SKILL: Caring

ATTACK: Fullswing

SOULTIMATE MOVE: Pick-a-Present

INSPIRIT: So Generous

TECHNIQUE: Restore

FAVORITE FOOD: Milk

EASINESS TO BEFRIEND: ★★★

EVOLUTION: NO EVOLUTIONS ✱ **FUSION:** NO FUSIONS

NUMBER
129

HEARTFUL

OL' FORTUNE

Another old man with bags full of gifts. Unlike Ol' Saint Trick, all of his presents are good!

STATS

SKILL: Penetrate

ATTACK: Fullswing

SOULTIMATE MOVE: Get-a-Present

INSPIRIT: So Generous

TECHNIQUE: Lightning

FAVORITE FOOD: Milk

EASINESS TO BEFRIEND: ★★★

EVOLUTION: NO EVOLUTIONS * **FUSION:** NO FUSIONS

HEARTFUL

ROLLEN

Everything he does is decided by a roll of his dice eyes. Their outcome changes his personality!

STATS

SKILL: Gambler

ATTACK: Earthsplitter

SOULTIMATE MOVE: Roll of Fate

INSPIRIT: Luck's Smile

TECHNIQUE: Rapids

FAVORITE FOOD: Candy

EASINESS TO BEFRIEND: ★★★

EVOLUTION: NO EVOLUTIONS ✻ **FUSION:** NO FUSIONS

NUMBER 131

HEARTFUL

DUBBLES

Dubbles will inspirit you and point you toward an unknown fate. Even he doesn't know if it'll be a good or bad one.

STATS

SKILL: Gambler

ATTACK: Earthsplitter

SOULTIMATE MOVE: Hit It Big!

INSPIRIT: Lucky Streak

TECHNIQUE: Waterfall

FAVORITE FOOD: Candy

EASINESS TO BEFRIEND: ★★

EVOLUTION: NO EVOLUTIONS * **FUSION:** NO FUSIONS

NUMBER 132

HEARTFUL

PAPA BOLT

No matter how lazy you are, you'll work quickly when Papa Bolt's watching. His anger is SCAAAAARY!

STATS

SKILL: Strict

ATTACK: Practiced Punch

SOULTIMATE MOVE: A Father's Scorn

INSPIRIT: Dad's Support

TECHNIQUE: Lightning

FAVORITE FOOD: Meat

EASINESS TO BEFRIEND: ★★★

EVOLUTION: NO EVOLUTIONS * **FUSION:** NO FUSIONS

RARE!

UNCLE INFINITE

RARE! Even Papa Bolt is scared of Uncle Infinite's power. He can throw a table an entire mile!

STATS

SKILL: Intimidation

ATTACK: Practiced Punch

SOULTIMATE MOVE: Table Flip

INSPIRIT: Uncle's Shout

TECHNIQUE: Voltage

FAVORITE FOOD: Meat

EASINESS TO BEFRIEND: 

EVOLUTION: NO EVOLUTIONS * **FUSION:** NO FUSIONS

NUMBER
134

HEARTFUL

MAMA AURA

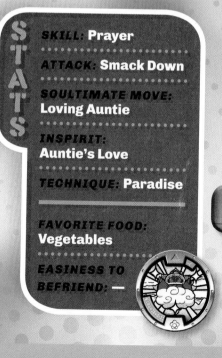

Sometimes strict and sometimes nice, she embraces Yo-kai with her warm aura. No Yo-kai can defy her.

STATS

SKILL: Prayer

ATTACK: Smack Down

SOULTIMATE MOVE: A Mother's Love

INSPIRIT: Mama's Warmth

TECHNIQUE: Paradise

FAVORITE FOOD: Vegetables

EASINESS TO BEFRIEND: ★★

EVOLUTION: NO EVOLUTIONS * **FUSION:** NO FUSIONS

NUMBER
135

HEARTFUL

AUNTIE HEART

Regardless of how bad a Yo-kai is, Auntie Heart's healing hug will make them pure again. That is some true kindness!

STATS

SKILL: Prayer

ATTACK: Smack Down

SOULTIMATE MOVE: Loving Auntie

INSPIRIT: Auntie's Love

TECHNIQUE: Paradise

FAVORITE FOOD: Vegetables

EASINESS TO BEFRIEND: —

EVOLUTION: NO EVOLUTIONS * **FUSION:** NO FUSIONS

SHADY

LEADONI

A Yo-kai who beckons people with his huge hand and gets them confused. It's his fault when a child gets lost!

SKILL: Windshield

ATTACK: Slap

SOULTIMATE MOVE: C'mon This Way!

INSPIRIT: Guide

TECHNIQUE: Hail

FAVORITE FOOD: Candy

EASINESS TO BEFRIEND: ★★★★

EVOLUTION: NO EVOLUTIONS * **FUSION:** NO FUSIONS

NUMBER
137

SHADY

MYNIMO

A person inspirited by Mynimo gets much better treatment than those around them. Hey! That's not fair!

STATS

SKILL: Windshield

ATTACK: Slap

SOULTIMATE MOVE: Just for You

INSPIRIT: Bias

TECHNIQUE: Absorb

FAVORITE FOOD: Candy

EASINESS TO BEFRIEND: ★★★★

EVOLUTION: NO EVOLUTIONS * **FUSION:** NO FUSIONS

IN THE VIDEO GAME:

A bratty Yo-kai who is always kicking people's shoulders. His kicks just make your shoulders stiff.

IN THE ANIMATION:

Ake and his master, Payn, deliver stiff necks and sore shoulders to people by hammering away on their neck and shoulders. In one morning, they hit Nate's dad and all of Nate's friends!

STATS

SKILL: Extreme Critical

ATTACK: Kick

SOULTIMATE MOVE: Shoulder Crunch

INSPIRIT: Shoulder Pain

TECHNIQUE: Pebble

CATCHPHRASE: "Yes sir, Mr. Payn, sir!"

FAVORITE FOOD: Candy

EASINESS TO BEFRIEND:

EVOLUTION: NO EVOLUTIONS * **FUSION:** NO FUSIONS

IN THE VIDEO GAME:

Payn will show your shoulders the meaning of pain using his massive strength. Payn is really into working out.

IN THE ANIMATION:

Nate begged Payn and Ake to give him sore shoulders, just like all his friends. Together Ake and Payn hammered Nate's shoulders until they were totally exhausted. But according to Payn, Nate was just too loose and lazy.

STATS

SKILL: Extreme Critical

ATTACK: Power Punch

SOULTIMATE MOVE: Shoulder Lock

INSPIRIT: Shoulder Pain

TECHNIQUE: Rockslide

CATCHPHRASE: "Let's get to work Keke boy!"

FAVORITE FOOD: Candy

EASINESS TO BEFRIEND: ★★★

EVOLUTION: NO EVOLUTIONS * **FUSION:**

Ake + Buff Weight = Payn

NUMBER
140

AGON

SHADY

RARE! A horrible Yo-kai who gives people slipped discs in their backs! You're more susceptible the older you are.

STATS

SKILL: Extreme Critical

ATTACK: Power Punch

SOULTIMATE MOVE: Backache Buster

INSPIRIT: Back Pain

TECHNIQUE: Meteor

FAVORITE FOOD: Candy

EASINESS TO BEFRIEND: ★★★

EVOLUTION: NO EVOLUTIONS * **FUSION:** NO FUSIONS

NEGATIBUZZ

STATS

SKILL: Vampiric

ATTACK: Pesky Poke

SOULTIMATE MOVE: Negativity Germs

INSPIRIT: Negativize

TECHNIQUE: Absorb

FAVORITE FOOD: Juice

EASINESS TO BEFRIEND: ★★★★★

IN THE VIDEO GAME:

A Yo-kai who loves human negativity, he nurtures negativity, which he drinks with his needlelike nose.

IN THE ANIMATION:

Negatibuzz filled Nate's dentist with doubt, making him obsess about what could go wrong. Nate had to summon Blazion to pump the dentist back up.

EVOLUTION: NO EVOLUTIONS

FUSION: NO FUSIONS

MOSKEVIL

STATS

SKILL: Vampiric

ATTACK: Pinpoint Pierce

SOULTIMATE MOVE: Think Evil

INSPIRIT: Negativize

TECHNIQUE: Drain

FAVORITE FOOD: Juice

EASINESS TO BEFRIEND: ★★★

This nasty Yo-kai can drop you into the depths of despair. You cannot cheer up if he's nearby.

EVOLUTION:

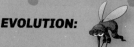

Negatibuzz level 17 ⇛ Moskevil

FUSION: NO FUSIONS

SCRITCHY

SHADY

RARE! **The mere presence of Scritchy will make your body itch. No amount of scratching can make it stop.**

STATS

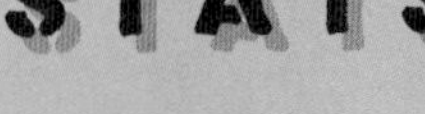

SKILL: Vampiric

ATTACK: Pinpoint Pierce

SOULTIMATE MOVE: Itchpocalypse

INSPIRIT: Itchy

TECHNIQUE: Voltage

FAVORITE FOOD: Juice

EASINESS TO BEFRIEND: ★★★

EVOLUTION: NO EVOLUTIONS ✱ **FUSION:** NO FUSIONS

NUMBER 144

SHADY

TV SEASON 1

DIMMY

SKILL: Secrecy

ATTACK: Stepping Slice

SOULTIMATE MOVE: Did You See Me?

INSPIRIT: Fade Away

TECHNIQUE: Whirlwind

CATCHPHRASE: "It's okay, don't worry about me."

FAVORITE FOOD: Rice Balls

EASINESS TO BEFRIEND: ★★★★

IN THE VIDEO GAME:

Being inspirited by Dimmy will tone down your presence. Dimmy uses this for his job as a ninja.

IN THE ANIMATION:

Nate became a shadow of his former self when Dimmy inspirited him. Nate was okay with that . . . until Whisper helped him collide with Dazzabel.

EVOLUTION: NO EVOLUTIONS

FUSION: NO FUSIONS

NUMBER 145

SHADY

BLANDON

SKILL: Secrecy

ATTACK: Ninja Star

SOULTIMATE MOVE: Hazy Dance

INSPIRIT: Fade Away

TECHNIQUE: Tornado

FAVORITE FOOD: Rice Balls

EASINESS TO BEFRIEND: ★★★

Blandon's lack of presence makes him a really great spy, but he's sad that no one recognizes him for that.

EVOLUTION:

Dimmy level 24 ⇛ Blandon

FUSION: NO FUSIONS

NUMBER
146

SHADY

NUL

You can't sense Nul even if you're really close to him. He's really good at entertaining himself.

STATS

SKILL: Secrecy

ATTACK: Ninja Star

SOULTIMATE MOVE: Creep 'n' Cut

INSPIRIT: Absence

TECHNIQUE: Storm

FAVORITE FOOD: Rice Balls

EASINESS TO BEFRIEND: ★★★

EVOLUTION: *NO EVOLUTIONS* ✻ **FUSION:** *NO FUSIONS*

NUMBER
147

SHADY

HIDABAT

STATS

SKILL: Vampiric

ATTACK: Slap

SOULTIMATE MOVE: Hidabat Harmony

INSPIRIT: Shut Away

TECHNIQUE: Tornado

FAVORITE FOOD: Meat

EASINESS TO BEFRIEND: ★★★★

IN THE VIDEO GAME:

Hidabat will make you a shut-in who fears going outside. He's better at inspiriting modern city dwellers.

IN THE ANIMATION:

Hidabat seeks seclusion, but the world is too scary to hide all alone. Luckily, Hidabat is happy to rent Nate's closet.

EVOLUTION: *NO EVOLUTIONS* ✻ **FUSION:** *NO FUSIONS*

NUMBER 148

SHADY

ABODABAT

After being inside the house for so long, Hidabat fused with it. Now it really can't ever leave!

STATS

SKILL: Vampiric

ATTACK: Tackle

SOULTIMATE MOVE: Abodaballad

INSPIRIT: Shut Away

TECHNIQUE: Tornado

FAVORITE FOOD: Meat

EASINESS TO BEFRIEND:

EVOLUTION: NO EVOLUTIONS * **FUSION:**

Hidabat + Tengloom = Abodabat

RARE!

BELFREE

RARE! A rare Abodabat in temporary housing. Once a year, if you're lucky, you can see him change houses.

STATS

SKILL: Vampiric

ATTACK: Tackle

SOULTIMATE MOVE: Belfree Blues

INSPIRIT: Shut Away

TECHNIQUE: Storm

FAVORITE FOOD: Meat

EASINESS TO BEFRIEND: 

EVOLUTION: NO EVOLUTIONS * **FUSION:** NO FUSIONS

NUMBER 150

SHADY

TV SEASON 2

SUSPICIONI

An Oni who doubts everything. He hangs out with his fellow Oni, but doesn't trust them at all.

STATS

SKILL: Suspicion

ATTACK: Pinpoint Pierce

SOULTIMATE MOVE: Suspicious Eyes

INSPIRIT: Distrust

TECHNIQUE: Torrent

FAVORITE FOOD: Chinese Food

EASINESS TO BEFRIEND: ★★★★

EVOLUTION: NO EVOLUTIONS * **FUSION:** NO FUSIONS

NUMBER 151

SHADY

STATS

SKILL: Suspicion

ATTACK: Pinpoint Pierce

SOULTIMATE MOVE: Temper Tantrum

INSPIRIT: Bratty

TECHNIQUE: Fire

FAVORITE FOOD: Chinese Food

EASINESS TO BEFRIEND: ★★★★★

TANTRONI

This Yo-kai will throw a fit whenever he doesn't get his way . . . It's probably time to grow out of that.

EVOLUTION: NO EVOLUTIONS * **FUSION:** NO FUSIONS

NUMBER 152

SHADY

SKILL: Suspicion

ATTACK: Pinpoint Pierce

SOULTIMATE MOVE: Contrary Gas

INSPIRIT: Contrariness

TECHNIQUE: Lightning

FAVORITE FOOD: Chinese Food

EASINESS TO BEFRIEND: ★★★

CONTRARIONI

Get ready to say no a lot if Contrarioni inspirits you. You'll disagree with anything people say. Always fun at parties.

EVOLUTION: NO EVOLUTIONS
FUSION: NO FUSIONS

SKILL: Windshield

ATTACK: Flip Kick

SOULTIMATE MOVE: Gloomy Storm

INSPIRIT: Pessimism

TECHNIQUE: Tornado

CATCHPHRASE: "Whatever. Who cares."

FAVORITE FOOD: Vegetables

EASINESS TO BEFRIEND: ★★★★

TV SEASONS 1 AND 2

NUMBER 153

SHADY

TENGLOOM

IN THE VIDEO GAME:

A gloomy Tengu who's always reading. He's somehow amassed a Yo-kai fan base that likes his pessimism.

IN THE ANIMATION:

Tengloom controls the winds of apathy and despair. He is the Yo-kai who lets you know when the party is over. He also invented kale chips.

EVOLUTION: NO EVOLUTIONS ✳ **FUSION:** NO FUSIONS

NUMBER 154

SHADY

NIRD

This Yo-kai became a bookworm when he came to the human world. Noisiness will be severely punished! Shhhh!

STATS

SKILL: Death Sphere

ATTACK: Flip Kick

SOULTIMATE MOVE: Demonic Storm

INSPIRIT: Stygian Curse

TECHNIQUE: Storm

FAVORITE FOOD: Vegetables

EASINESS TO BEFRIEND: ★★★

EVOLUTION: NO EVOLUTIONS ✱ **FUSION:** NO FUSIONS

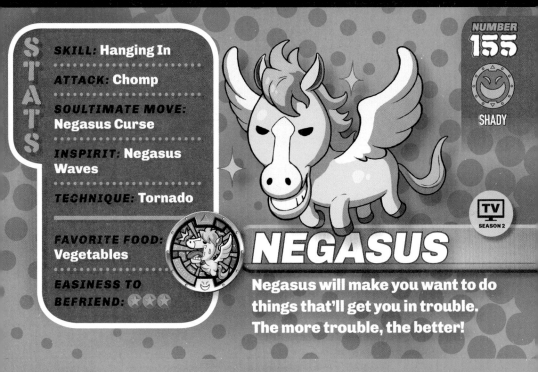

NUMBER 155

SHADY

STATS

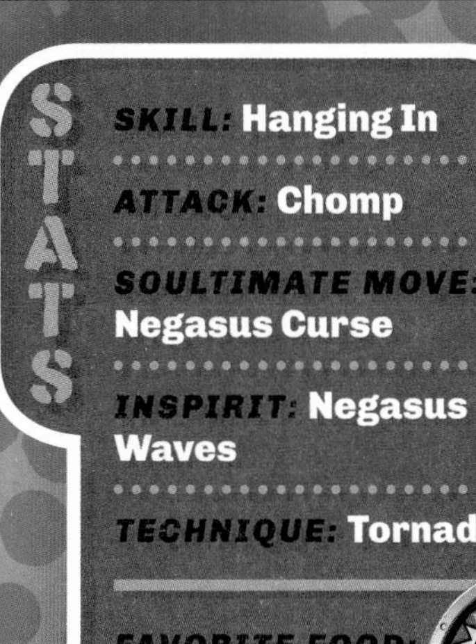

SKILL: Hanging In

ATTACK: Chomp

SOULTIMATE MOVE: Negasus Curse

INSPIRIT: Negasus Waves

TECHNIQUE: Tornado

FAVORITE FOOD: Vegetables

EASINESS TO BEFRIEND: ★★★

TV SEASON 2

NEGASUS

Negasus will make you want to do things that'll get you in trouble. The more trouble, the better!

EVOLUTION: NO EVOLUTIONS ✱ **FUSION:** NO FUSIONS

NUMBER
156

SHADY

NEIGHFARIOUS

RARE! Shining mysteriously in the night sky, Neighfarious is a bit of an enigma. What kind of evil Yo-kai is he?

STATS

SKILL: Cursed Skin

ATTACK: Chomp

SOULTIMATE MOVE: Dark Horse

INSPIRIT: Neighing Curse

TECHNIQUE: Drain

FAVORITE FOOD: Vegetables

EASINESS TO BEFRIEND: 

EVOLUTION: NO EVOLUTIONS * **FUSION:** NO FUSIONS

TIMIDEVIL

A nervous devil who's too scared to even use his own powers. If he'd just relax, he could be unstoppable.

STATS

SKILL: Too Afraid

ATTACK: Stab Storm

SOULTIMATE MOVE: Timid Boo

INSPIRIT: Scaredy-Cat

TECHNIQUE: Blaze

FAVORITE FOOD: Ramen

EASINESS TO BEFRIEND: ★★★★

EVOLUTION: NO EVOLUTIONS * **FUSION:** NO FUSIONS

NUMBER
158
SHADY

TV SEASON 2

BEELZEBOLD

Timidevil at full power! He still gets nervous every so often though.

STATS

SKILL: Intimidation

ATTACK: Stab Storm

SOULTIMATE MOVE: Boldakazam

INSPIRIT: Scaredy-Cat

TECHNIQUE: Incinerate

FAVORITE FOOD: Ramen

EASINESS TO BEFRIEND: ★★★

EVOLUTION: NO EVOLUTIONS * **FUSION:**

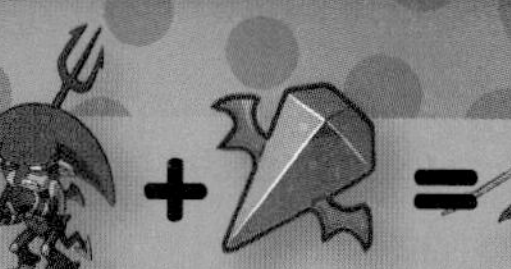

Timidevil + Shard of Evil = Beelzebold

RARE!

NUMBER 159

COUNT CAVITY

SHADY

RARE! A terrifying Yo-kai who can dissolve your teeth. He loves the sound of kids crying over aching teeth. What a jerk.

STATS

SKILL: Extreme Critical

ATTACK: Stab Storm

SOULTIMATE MOVE: Bacteria Barrage

INSPIRIT: Cavity

TECHNIQUE: Incinerate

FAVORITE FOOD: Ramen

EASINESS TO BEFRIEND: —

EVOLUTION: NO EVOLUTIONS * **FUSION:** NO FUSIONS

GREESEL

SHADY

TV SEASON 2

A powerful, greedy Yo-kai who wants to control the world's wealth. He'll do anything for money.

STATS

SKILL: **Mine**

ATTACK: **Clobber**

SOULTIMATE MOVE: **Stingy Curse**

INSPIRIT: **Stinginess**

TECHNIQUE: **Blaze**

FAVORITE FOOD: **Meat**

EASINESS TO BEFRIEND: ★★

EVOLUTION: ***NO EVOLUTIONS*** * ***FUSION:*** ***NO FUSIONS***

NUMBER 161

AWEVIL

SHADY

RARE! An aristocrat of evil. Pure depravity. A Yo-kai who will do anything just because it's bad. He's earned his name.

SKILL: Ultimate Darkness

ATTACK: Clobber

SOULTIMATE MOVE: Pitch-Black Curse

INSPIRIT: Darkness Power

TECHNIQUE: Rapids

FAVORITE FOOD: Meat

EASINESS TO BEFRIEND: 

EVOLUTION: NO EVOLUTIONS ✱ **FUSION:** NO FUSIONS

NUMBER 162

EERIE

TV SEASON 1

COUGHKOFF

SKILL: Spikey Guard

ATTACK: Pesky Poke

SOULTIMATE MOVE: Koff Dropper

INSPIRIT: Sore Throat

TECHNIQUE: Torrent

CATCHPHRASE: "Cough..."

FAVORITE FOOD: Bread

EASINESS TO BEFRIEND: ★★★★★

IN THE VIDEO GAME:

Coughkoff can make your throat feel tingly and make you sick. Try to stay healthy!

IN THE ANIMATION:

Together with Duchoo, Coughkoff helped Nate fake a sick day and skip school. Unfortunately, Nate soon came down with a real cold!

EVOLUTION: *NO EVOLUTIONS*

FUSION: *NO FUSIONS*

NUMBER 163

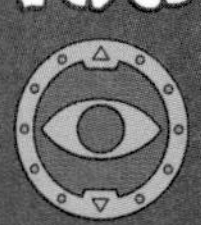

EERIE

SKILL: Spikey Guard

ATTACK: Pesky Poke

SOULTIMATE MOVE: Sting Bomb

INSPIRIT: Headache

TECHNIQUE: Frost

FAVORITE FOOD: Bread

EASINESS TO BEFRIEND: ★★★★

HURCHIN

He looks just like Coughkoff, but don't say that! He hates that guy.

EVOLUTION: *NO EVOLUTIONS* **FUSION:** *NO FUSIONS*

NUMBER 164

EERIE

TV SEASONS 1 AND 2

PECKPOCKET

IN THE VIDEO GAME:

When Peckpocket has his eye on you, you'll start wanting other people's stuff. I'll take that!

IN THE ANIMATION:

Peckpocket makes people want to take things. When Peckpocket inspirited Bear, Nate summoned Roughraff, but the two Yo-kai got along a little *too* well.

STATS

SKILL: Glossy Skin

ATTACK: Squish

SOULTIMATE MOVE: Life Snag

INSPIRIT: Snatch

TECHNIQUE: Absorb

CATCHPHRASE: "What's yours is mine, mine, all mine."

FAVORITE FOOD: Hamburger

EASINESS TO BEFRIEND:

EVOLUTION: NO EVOLUTIONS

FUSION: NO FUSIONS

NUMBER 165

EERIE

TV SEASON 1

ROCKABELLY

IN THE VIDEO GAME:

A weird Yo-kai who is quite the belly dancer. His stomach feathers look like an old man's face.

IN THE ANIMATION:

Rockabelly makes a funny face appear on your belly—and then gives you the irresistible urge to make it dance.

STATS

SKILL: Glossy Skin

ATTACK: Squish

SOULTIMATE MOVE: Face Flop

INSPIRIT: Funky Dance

TECHNIQUE: Drain

CATCHPHRASE: "Ready?"

FAVORITE FOOD: Hamburger

EASINESS TO BEFRIEND:

EVOLUTION: NO EVOLUTIONS

FUSION: NO FUSIONS

BUHU

IN THE VIDEO GAME:

This bird Yo-kai is always bummed out. People she inspirits get depressed and distracted a lot.

STATS

SKILL: Wind Play

ATTACK: Pesky Poke

SOULTIMATE MOVE: Boo Hoo Blast

INSPIRIT: Depression

TECHNIQUE: Whirlwind

CATCHPHRASE: "Boo, hoo, hoo!"

FAVORITE FOOD: Bread

EASINESS TO BEFRIEND:

IN THE ANIMATION:

Buhu gives people a false feeling of good fortune, and then, at the last second, she makes them feel dreadful. Nate thinks she looks a little creepy, but she can't help it.

EVOLUTION: *NO EVOLUTIONS*
FUSION: *NO FUSIONS*

FLUMPY

STATS

SKILL: Wind Play

ATTACK: Pesky Poke

SOULTIMATE MOVE: Awfully Awkward

INSPIRIT: Awkwardness

TECHNIQUE: Tornado

FAVORITE FOOD: Bread

EASINESS TO BEFRIEND:

Flumpy can make even the coolest person unfashionable and awkward. He hates being so unstylish.

EVOLUTION: *NO EVOLUTIONS* **FUSION:** *NO FUSIONS*

RARE!

NUMBER 168

EERIE

SKREEK

RARE! If you catch a glimpse of Skreek, just run. He can throw you into the deepest pits of despair.

STATS

SKILL: Penetrate

ATTACK: Pesky Poke

SOULTIMATE MOVE: Meet the Reaper

INSPIRIT: Despair

TECHNIQUE: Tornado

FAVORITE FOOD: Bread

EASINESS TO BEFRIEND: ★★★

EVOLUTION: NO EVOLUTIONS * **FUSION:** NO FUSIONS

TV SEASONS 1 AND 2

MANJIMUTT

IN THE VIDEO GAME:
A man-faced dog who enjoys scaring those who approach him expecting a regular poodle. Hopes to one day be a CEO.

IN THE ANIMATION:
Once upon a time, an average businessman was fired from his job. He collided with a poodle and some falling planks of wood, and he became Manjimutt.

STATS

SKILL: Mutt(man) Paradise

ATTACK: Chomp

SOULTIMATE MOVE: Creepy Superbite

INSPIRIT: Confusion

TECHNIQUE: Fire

CATCHPHRASE: "I'm just a dog!"

FAVORITE FOOD: Chinese Food

EASINESS TO BEFRIEND: ★★★★★

EVOLUTION: NO EVOLUTIONS

FUSION: NO FUSIONS

NUMBER 170

EERIE

MULTIMUTT

Nobody wants to get close to Multimutt because both of his faces look mean. He's a perfect guard dog.

STATS

SKILL: Mutt(man) Paradise

ATTACK: Chomp

SOULTIMATE MOVE: Superbite Twin

INSPIRIT: Confusion

TECHNIQUE: Blaze

FAVORITE FOOD: Chinese Food

EASINESS TO BEFRIEND: ★★★

EVOLUTION: NO EVOLUTIONS

FUSION:

Manjimutt + Manjimutt = Multimutt

RARE!

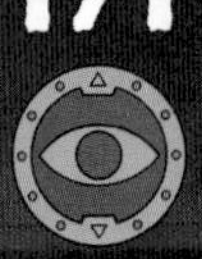

SIR BERUS

RARE! An elite guard dog born and raised in the netherworld. He doesn't let a single soul escape his grasp.

STATS

SKILL: Mutt(man) Paradise

ATTACK: Chomp

SOULTIMATE MOVE: Stygian Slingshot

INSPIRIT: Styx's Curse

TECHNIQUE: Meteor

FAVORITE FOOD: Chinese Food

EASINESS TO BEFRIEND:  

EVOLUTION: NO EVOLUTIONS * **FUSION:** NO FUSIONS

NUMBER
172

EERIE

DROPLETTE

Droplette makes his way to places that don't get much sun and makes them damp and moldy . . . Gross.

SKILL: Moist Skin

ATTACK: Body Bash

SOULTIMATE MOVE: Drizzling Shower

INSPIRIT: Pruned

TECHNIQUE: Torrent

FAVORITE FOOD: Juice

EASINESS TO BEFRIEND: ★★★★★

STATS

EVOLUTION: NO EVOLUTIONS ✱ **FUSION:** NO FUSIONS

TV SEASON 1

NUMBER
173

EERIE

DRIZZLE

SKILL: Moist Skin

ATTACK: Body Bash

SOULTIMATE MOVE: Heavy Squall

INSPIRIT: Pruned

TECHNIQUE: Rapids

FAVORITE FOOD: Juice

EASINESS TO BEFRIEND: ★★★

STATS

IN THE VIDEO GAME:

Drizzle creates rain clouds wherever he goes. You can find him in places that are thoroughly wet.

IN THE ANIMATION:

Drizzle rolled in on Nate's family's spring break. Fortunately, once Robonyan got rid of him, there was a rainbow to lighten the mood.

EVOLUTION:

Droplette level 25 ⇛ Drizzle

FUSION: NO FUSIONS

NUMBER
174

EERIE

SLUSH

A large gathering of these frosty Yo-kai could freeze anything. Just one can freeze a cup of water.

STATS

SKILL: Stiff Skin

ATTACK: Body Bash

SOULTIMATE MOVE: Shivering Sigh

INSPIRIT: Numbify

TECHNIQUE: Hail

FAVORITE FOOD: Juice

EASINESS TO BEFRIEND: ★★★★

EVOLUTION: NO EVOLUTIONS

FUSION: NO FUSIONS

NUMBER
175

EERIE

ALHAIL

This Yo-kai has strong ice power by itself. Ice will gradually encase whatever he touches.

STATS

SKILL: Stiff Skin

ATTACK: Body Bash

SOULTIMATE MOVE: Heavenly Hail

INSPIRIT: Frozen Solid

TECHNIQUE: Frost

FAVORITE FOOD: Juice

EASINESS TO BEFRIEND: ★★★

EVOLUTION:

Slush level 25 ⇛ Alhail

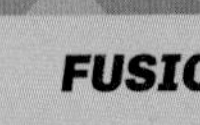

FUSION: NO FUSIONS

GUSH

RARE!

RARE! If he inspirits you, your nose won't stop bleeding. This Yo-kai can be much scarier than he looks.

TV SEASON 2

STATS

SKILL: Good Fortune

ATTACK: Body Bash

SOULTIMATE MOVE: Nosebleed Bomb

INSPIRIT: Nosebleed

TECHNIQUE: Blaze

FAVORITE FOOD: Juice

EASINESS TO BEFRIEND: 

EVOLUTION: NO EVOLUTIONS * **FUSION:** NO FUSIONS

NUMBER 177

EERIE

CHATALIE

IN THE VIDEO GAME:

All talk and no action. If she inspirits you, you'll be the same and lose the trust of others.

IN THE ANIMATION:

This loudmouth Yo-kai pumps people full of hot air and causes them to brag shamelessly. She's to blame for most politicians' campaign promises.

STATS

SKILL: Skilled Loafer

ATTACK: Bite

SOULTIMATE MOVE: Bigmouth

INSPIRIT: All Talk

TECHNIQUE: Shock

CATCHPHRASE: "If you've got it, flaunt it."

FAVORITE FOOD: Bread

EASINESS TO BEFRIEND: ★★★★

EVOLUTION: NO EVOLUTIONS

FUSION: NO FUSIONS

NUMBER 178

EERIE

NAGATHA

Nagatha will make you into the kind of person who'll nag people over the smallest mistake.

STATS

SKILL: Skilled Loafer

ATTACK: Bite

SOULTIMATE MOVE: Badger Bite

INSPIRIT: Complaints

TECHNIQUE: Drain

FAVORITE FOOD: Bread

EASINESS TO BEFRIEND: ★★★★

EVOLUTION: NO EVOLUTIONS * **FUSION:** NO FUSIONS

NUMBER 179

EERIE

TV SEASONS 1 AND 2

DISMARELDA

IN THE VIDEO GAME:
Her gloomy aura can darken the mood in any environment. It's even worse when she's in a bad mood.

IN THE ANIMATION:
This Yo-kai creates conflict wherever she goes. Dismarelda made Nate's parents fight over yogurt!

STATS

SKILL: Cursed Skin

ATTACK: Squish

SOULTIMATE MOVE: Dismartillery

INSPIRIT: Overcast

TECHNIQUE: Pebble

CATCHPHRASE: "No filter."

FAVORITE FOOD: Bread

EASINESS TO BEFRIEND: ★★★★

EVOLUTION: NO EVOLUTIONS
FUSION: NO FUSIONS

STATS

SKILL: Gassy Sphere

ATTACK: Headbutt

SOULTIMATE MOVE: Stinky Smog

INSPIRIT: Stink Up

TECHNIQUE: Frost

CATCHPHRASE: "Poo-poo!"

FAVORITE FOOD: Milk

EASINESS TO BEFRIEND: ★★★★★

TV SEASONS 1 AND 2

NUMBER 180

EERIE

CHEEKSQUEEK

A Yo-kai who can't stop farting. There's a rumor that he just has really bad breath . . . but I'm not going to clear the air here.

EVOLUTION: NO EVOLUTIONS * **FUSION:** NO FUSIONS

TV SEASON 2

SKILL: Sense of Smell

ATTACK: Headbutt

SOULTIMATE MOVE: Toxic Gas

INSPIRIT: Stink Up

TECHNIQUE: Frost

FAVORITE FOOD: Milk

EASINESS TO BEFRIEND: ★★★

STATS

CUTTINCHEEZ

A god of flatulence. Brace yourself for an agonizing death if you get stuck in a windowless room with Cuttincheez.

EVOLUTION: NO EVOLUTIONS * **FUSION:** NO FUSIONS

STATS

SKILL: Hanging In

ATTACK: Beat

SOULTIMATE MOVE: Lamest Joke

INSPIRIT: Fall Flat

TECHNIQUE: Drain

FAVORITE FOOD: Chinese Food

EASINESS TO BEFRIEND: ★★★

COMPUNZER

Even though he wants to make people laugh, Compunzer's jokes fall flat and just lead to awkward silences.

EVOLUTION: NO EVOLUTIONS * **FUSION:** NO FUSIONS

NUMBER 183

EERIE

LAMEDIAN

His jokes are the worst, only inciting involuntary guffaws at best. But he thinks he's hilarious. IS HE RIGHT, FOLKS?!

STATS

SKILL: Hanging In

ATTACK: Beat

SOULTIMATE MOVE: Millennium of Lame

INSPIRIT: Fall Flat

TECHNIQUE: Reaper

FAVORITE FOOD: Chinese Food

EASINESS TO BEFRIEND: ★★

EVOLUTION: NO EVOLUTIONS * **FUSION:** NO FUSIONS

NUMBER 184

EERIE

TV SEASON 2

GRUMPLES

Bitter toward youth and beauty, Grumples makes people wrinkly. She was quite the beauty when she was young, though.

STATS

SKILL: Oldness Zone

ATTACK: Hit

SOULTIMATE MOVE: Scary Wrinkles

INSPIRIT: Wrinkles

TECHNIQUE: Absorb

FAVORITE FOOD: Milk

EASINESS TO BEFRIEND: ★★★

EVOLUTION: NO EVOLUTIONS * **FUSION:** NO FUSIONS

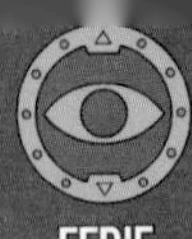

EVERFORE

TV SEASON 2

Sustaining her own youth and beauty by absorbing it from others, Everfore is always on the hunt for beautiful women.

STATS

SKILL: Oldness Zone

ATTACK: Beat

SOULTIMATE MOVE: Beauty Beam

INSPIRIT: Youth Drain

TECHNIQUE: Reaper

FAVORITE FOOD: Milk

EASINESS TO BEFRIEND: —

EVOLUTION: NO EVOLUTIONS * **FUSION:**

 +  = 

Grumples + Ageless Powder = Everfore

NUMBER 186

EERIE

ETERNA

RARE!

RARE!

They say this Yo-kai's immortality stems from her staff and that she'll age instantly without it.

STATS

SKILL: Oldness Zone

ATTACK: Beat

SOULTIMATE MOVE: Undying Drain

INSPIRIT: Immortal Power

TECHNIQUE: Reaper

FAVORITE FOOD: Milk

EASINESS TO BEFRIEND: —

EVOLUTION: NO EVOLUTIONS * **FUSION:** NO FUSIONS

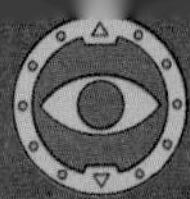

EERIE

INSOMNI

IN THE VIDEO GAME:

Catch Insomni's eye and she won't let you fall asleep until she's bored of you or until you're nearly dead.

IN THE ANIMATION:

Insomni makes people stay up too late and then regret it in the morning, when they're complete basket cases. In the case of Nate's teacher, this can lead to prattling on about éclairs for no apparent reason.

STATS

SKILL: Insecure

ATTACK: Smack Down

SOULTIMATE MOVE: Never Sleep Ever

INSPIRIT: Insomnia

TECHNIQUE: Blizzard

CATCHPHRASE: "Sleeping is no fun. Let's stay up all night long."

FAVORITE FOOD: Candy

EASINESS TO BEFRIEND: 

EVOLUTION: NO EVOLUTIONS * **FUSION:** NO FUSIONS

NUMBER 188

SANDI

EERIE

RARE!

RARE! When Sandi inspirits you, the two of you will play in your dreams . . . it's too fun to ever wake up from.

STATS

SKILL: I Have a Grip on You!

ATTACK: Smack Down

SOULTIMATE MOVE: Unwaking Dream

INSPIRIT: Bedtime

TECHNIQUE: Reaper

FAVORITE FOOD: Candy

EASINESS TO BEFRIEND: 

EVOLUTION: NO EVOLUTIONS * **FUSION:** NO FUSIONS

NUMBER 189

SLIPPERY

TV SEASONS 1 AND 2

NOKO

SKILL: Good Fortune

ATTACK: Bite

SOULTIMATE MOVE: Noko Smile

INSPIRIT: Fortunate

TECHNIQUE: Rockslide

CATCHPHRASE: "Noko, noko!"

FAVORITE FOOD: Hamburger

EASINESS TO BEFRIEND: ★★★

IN THE VIDEO GAME:

This Yo-kai is one lucky snake! He is always scared of being seen by humans. Which happens a lot, since he's terrible at hiding.

IN THE ANIMATION:

Noko is known for his amazing jumping ability. Whisper claims no one has ever seen one, and he gets super annoyed when Nate says he's seen a few.

EVOLUTION: *NO EVOLUTIONS*

FUSION: *NO FUSIONS*

NUMBER 190

SLIPPERY

BLOOMINOKO

SKILL: Good Fortune

ATTACK: Maul

SOULTIMATE MOVE: Lucky Smile

INSPIRIT: Fortunate

TECHNIQUE: Meteor

FAVORITE FOOD: Hamburger

EASINESS TO BEFRIEND: ★★

The flower on top of Bloominoko's head brings people luck and happiness. Some folks even worship him.

EVOLUTION: *NO EVOLUTIONS*

FUSION:  +  = 

Noko + Drop of Joy = Bloominoko

NUMBER 191

SLIPPERY

PANDANOKO

RARE!

RARE! A wandering Yo-kai from a faraway land. He's tough to find and a miracle to actually befriend.

STATS

SKILL: Summon

ATTACK: Maul

SOULTIMATE MOVE: Panda Smile

INSPIRIT: Panda Cuteness

TECHNIQUE: Frost

FAVORITE FOOD: Hamburger

EASINESS TO BEFRIEND: ★★★

EVOLUTION: NO EVOLUTIONS * **FUSION:** NO FUSIONS

NUMBER 192

SLIPPERY

TV SEASON 2

HEHEHEEL

This eel just can't stop laughing, and nobody knows why. Maybe its sense of humor is broken.

STATS

SKILL: Jar Guard

ATTACK: Chomp

SOULTIMATE MOVE: In Da Funny Bone

INSPIRIT: Playfulness

TECHNIQUE: Heal

CATCHPHRASE: "Makes me EL OH EL!"

FAVORITE FOOD: Meat

EASINESS TO BEFRIEND: ★★★★

EVOLUTION: NO EVOLUTIONS * **FUSION:** NO FUSIONS

STATS

SKILL: Jar Guard

ATTACK: Chomp

SOULTIMATE MOVE: Eel Life

INSPIRIT: Power of Song

TECHNIQUE: Absorb

FAVORITE FOOD: Meat

EASINESS TO BEFRIEND: ★★★★

NUMBER 193

SLIPPERY

CROONGER

A pot Yo-kai who sings a strange tune. If you hear singing coming from a pot, don't look into it!

EVOLUTION: NO EVOLUTIONS * **FUSION:** NO FUSIONS

NUMBER 194

SLIPPERY

URNACONDA

That's no regular pot—there's a huge snake inside! Some say this inspired the creation of the jack-in-the-box.

SKILL: Jar Guard

ATTACK: Chomp

SOULTIMATE MOVE: Venoconda

INSPIRIT: Serpent's Power

TECHNIQUE: Restore

FAVORITE FOOD: Meat

EASINESS TO BEFRIEND: ★★★

EVOLUTION: NO EVOLUTIONS * **FUSION:** NO FUSIONS

NUMBER 195

SLIPPERY

FISHPICABLE

Fishpicable only sees the bad in people and slaps things he hates with his tail. His tail is very busy.

SKILL: Waterproof

ATTACK: Slap

SOULTIMATE MOVE: Hateful Charge

INSPIRIT: Hateful

TECHNIQUE: Shock

FAVORITE FOOD: Meat

EASINESS TO BEFRIEND: ★★★★

EVOLUTION: NO EVOLUTIONS * **FUSION:** NO FUSIONS

NUMBER 196

SLIPPERY

RAGEON

Rageon holds grudges for no reason. If you wake up to see him standing next to your bed . . . RUN!

STATS

SKILL: Waterproof

ATTACK: Double Slice

SOULTIMATE MOVE: Vengeance

INSPIRIT: Detest

TECHNIQUE: Lightning

FAVORITE FOOD: Meat

EASINESS TO BEFRIEND: 

EVOLUTION:   

Fishpicable level 27 ⇛ Rageon

FUSION: ***NO FUSIONS***

NUMBER
197

SLIPPERY

TUNATIC

RARE!

RARE!

Tunatic will go on a rampage if he's criticized at all. He makes kids angry when they get guidance from adults.

STATS

SKILL: Fire Play

ATTACK: Double Slice

SOULTIMATE MOVE: Frenzied Rage

INSPIRIT: Frenzy

TECHNIQUE: Incinerate

FAVORITE FOOD: Meat

EASINESS TO BEFRIEND:

EVOLUTION: NO EVOLUTIONS * **FUSION:** NO FUSIONS

NUMBER 198

SLIPPERY

DRAGGIE

A dragon kid who wants attention. He can see the hidden strengths of others with the crystal ball on his head.

STATS

SKILL: Hard Worker

ATTACK: Headsmack

SOULTIMATE MOVE: Draggie Stone

INSPIRIT: Dragon Power

TECHNIQUE: Rockslide

FAVORITE FOOD: Chinese Food

EASINESS TO BEFRIEND: ★★★

EVOLUTION: NO EVOLUTIONS * **FUSION:** NO FUSIONS

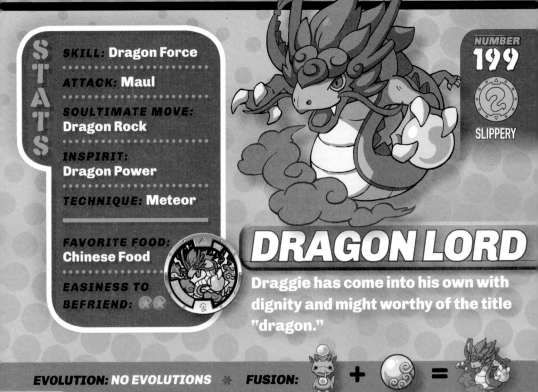

STATS

SKILL: Dragon Force

ATTACK: Maul

SOULTIMATE MOVE: Dragon Rock

INSPIRIT: Dragon Power

TECHNIQUE: Meteor

FAVORITE FOOD: Chinese Food

EASINESS TO BEFRIEND: ★★

NUMBER 199

SLIPPERY

DRAGON LORD

Draggie has come into his own with dignity and might worthy of the title "dragon."

EVOLUTION: NO EVOLUTIONS * **FUSION:**

 +  = 

Draggie + Dragon Orb = Dragon Lord

SLIPPERY

AZURE DRAGON

RARE!

RARE! A legendary divine beast. He holds domain over water, surpassing even the power of the Dragon Lord.

SKILL: Dragon Force

ATTACK: Maul

SOULTIMATE MOVE: Dragon Falls

INSPIRIT: Cobalt Power

TECHNIQUE: Waterfall

FAVORITE FOOD: Chinese Food

EASINESS TO BEFRIEND: ★★

EVOLUTION: NO EVOLUTIONS ✱ **FUSION:** NO FUSIONS

NUMBER
201

SLIPPERY

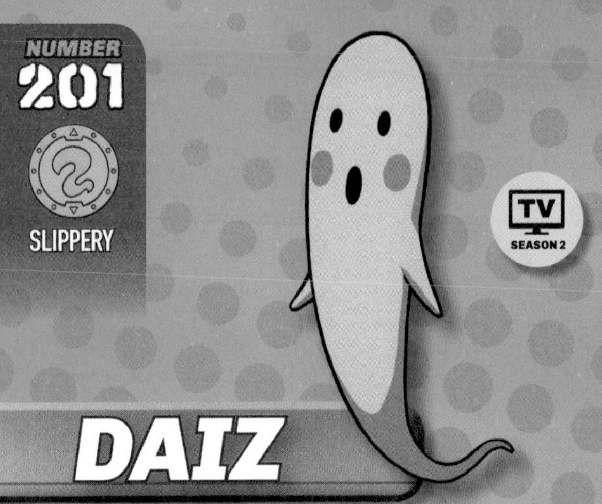

TV SEASON 2

DAIZ

Daiz just stares off into space, sometimes not moving for three whole days. What's it thinking about all that time . . . ?

STATS

SKILL: Dodge

ATTACK: Body Bash

SOULTIMATE MOVE: Spacing Out

INSPIRIT: Generous Heart

TECHNIQUE: Absorb

FAVORITE FOOD: Candy

EASINESS TO BEFRIEND: ★★★

EVOLUTION: NO EVOLUTIONS * **FUSION:** NO FUSIONS

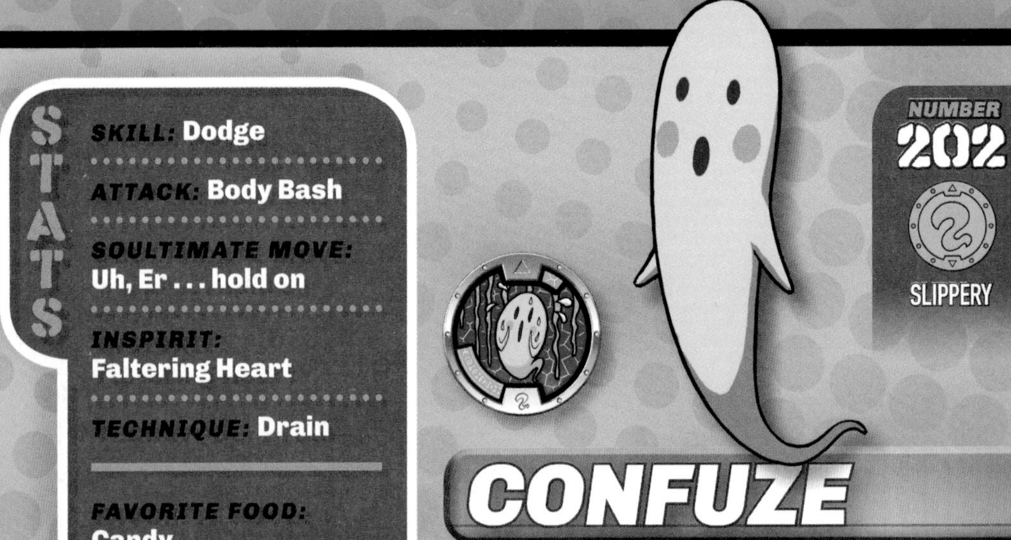

NUMBER
202

SLIPPERY

CONFUZE

Confuze will make you babble and mumble. It's the worst when you have to read out loud in class!

STATS

SKILL: Dodge

ATTACK: Body Bash

SOULTIMATE MOVE: Uh, Er . . . hold on

INSPIRIT: Faltering Heart

TECHNIQUE: Drain

FAVORITE FOOD: Candy

EASINESS TO BEFRIEND: ★★★

EVOLUTION: NO EVOLUTIONS * **FUSION:** NO FUSIONS

NUMBER 203

SLIPPERY

CHUMMER

Chummer loves eating kids. He'll make them loiter after school before devouring them. He likes asparagus, too.

SKILL: Loiterer

ATTACK: Maul

SOULTIMATE MOVE: Sharkskin Shield

INSPIRIT: Loitering

TECHNIQUE: Rapids

FAVORITE FOOD: Vegetables

EASINESS TO BEFRIEND:

EVOLUTION: NO EVOLUTIONS * **FUSION:** NO FUSIONS

SKILL: Shark Skin

ATTACK: Maul

SOULTIMATE MOVE: Feeding Frenzy

INSPIRIT: Amateur

TECHNIQUE: Waterfall

FAVORITE FOOD: Vegetables

EASINESS TO BEFRIEND:

TV SEASON 2

NUMBER 204

SLIPPERY

SHROOK

Shrook will make you bad at whatever you're usually good at. He can make a master into a novice pretty quickly.

EVOLUTION: NO EVOLUTIONS * **FUSION:** NO FUSIONS

NUMBER 205

SLIPPERY

SPENP

TV SEASONS 1 AND 2

IN THE VIDEO GAME:

Being inspirited by Spenp will make you buy things that you don't even want. Wave bye to your cash!

IN THE ANIMATION:

Spenp inspirited Nate and his friends and had them waste all their money on toilet paper and a giant fish instead of on the *YOLO Watch 2* game they wanted. Luckily, their purchases all came with raffle tickets for the game!

STATS

SKILL: Matchless Shell

ATTACK: Chomp

SOULTIMATE MOVE: Bank Breaker

INSPIRIT: Wastefulness

TECHNIQUE: Tornado

CATCHPHRASE: "I work hard and I play hard."

FAVORITE FOOD: Bread

EASINESS TO BEFRIEND: ★★★★★

EVOLUTION: NO EVOLUTIONS * **FUSION:** NO FUSIONS

SLIPPERY

ALMI

RARE!

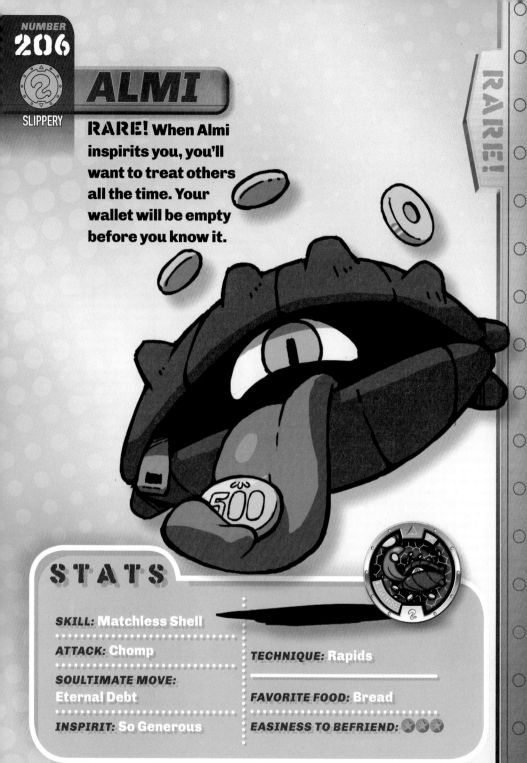

RARE! When Almi inspirits you, you'll want to treat others all the time. Your wallet will be empty before you know it.

STATS

SKILL: Matchless Shell

ATTACK: Chomp

SOULTIMATE MOVE: Eternal Debt

INSPIRIT: So Generous

TECHNIQUE: Rapids

FAVORITE FOOD: Bread

EASINESS TO BEFRIEND: ★★★

EVOLUTION: NO EVOLUTIONS ✱ **FUSION:** NO FUSIONS

SLIPPERY

BABBLONG

IN THE VIDEO GAME:

Don't agree to listen to Babblong or else he'll talk and talk and talk and talk and talk and talk and talk. He's a terrible listener.

IN THE ANIMATION:

Babblong makes people tell really long stories that go on forever. After inspiriting Nate's teacher and Katie, Babblong made Nate ramble on and on. Finally, Jibanyan had to trick Nate into summoning Wazzat to erase all of Babblong's stories.

STATS

SKILL: Skilled Loafer

ATTACK: Fullswing

SOULTIMATE MOVE: Babbleblast

INSPIRIT: Keep Chatting

TECHNIQUE: Rapids

CATCHPHRASE: "You know? You KNOW?"

FAVORITE FOOD: Candy

EASINESS TO BEFRIEND: ★★★★

EVOLUTION: NO EVOLUTIONS * **FUSION:** NO FUSIONS

NUMBER 208

SLIPPERY

BANANOSE

RARE!

RARE! This Yo-kai is made of banana and is often bothered by circling flies. No relation to Babblong.

STATS

SKILL: Skilled Loafer

ATTACK: Fullswing

SOULTIMATE MOVE: Banana Splat

INSPIRIT: Banana Power

TECHNIQUE: Waterfall

FAVORITE FOOD: Candy

EASINESS TO BEFRIEND: ★★★

EVOLUTION: NO EVOLUTIONS * **FUSION:** NO FUSIONS

NUMBER 209

SLIPPERY

TV SEASONS 1 AND 2

COPPERLED

You just can't refuse orders from the fan on this old Yo-kai's tail. And he loves to micromanage everything he can!

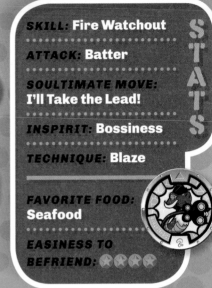

STATS

SKILL: Fire Watchout

ATTACK: Batter

SOULTIMATE MOVE: I'll Take the Lead!

INSPIRIT: Bossiness

TECHNIQUE: Blaze

FAVORITE FOOD: Seafood

EASINESS TO BEFRIEND: ★★★★

EVOLUTION: NO EVOLUTIONS ✻ **FUSION:** NO FUSIONS

STATS

SKILL: Greed

ATTACK: Batter

SOULTIMATE MOVE: Sulky Soul

INSPIRIT: Sulky

TECHNIQUE: Rapids

CATCHPHRASE: "Humph!"

FAVORITE FOOD: Seafood

EASINESS TO BEFRIEND: ★★★

NUMBER 210

SLIPPERY

TV SEASON 1

CYNAKE

IN THE VIDEO GAME:

This sulky snake Yo-kai will make you sulk at the slightest problem. Hmph!

IN THE ANIMATION:

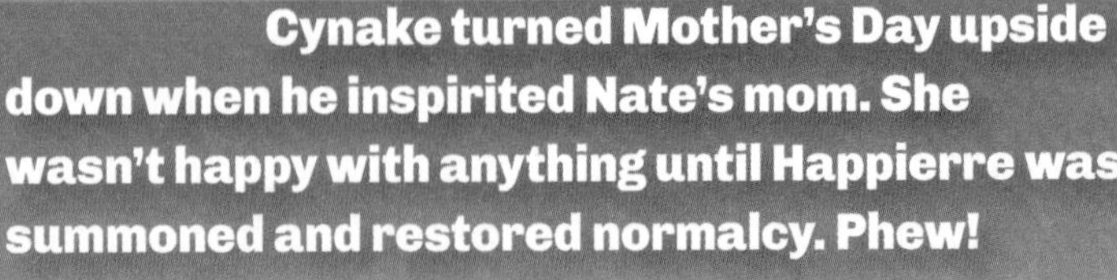

Cynake turned Mother's Day upside down when he inspirited Nate's mom. She wasn't happy with anything until Happierre was summoned and restored normalcy. Phew!

EVOLUTION: NO EVOLUTIONS ✻ **FUSION:** NO FUSIONS

NUMBER 211

SLIPPERY

SLITHEREF

When a battle starts, Slitheref will appear out of nowhere and make sure the fight stays fair and square.

STATS

SKILL: Equipment Forbidden!

ATTACK: Batter

SOULTIMATE MOVE: Venomous Feint

INSPIRIT: Pit Viper Venom

TECHNIQUE: Voltage

FAVORITE FOOD: Seafood

EASINESS TO BEFRIEND: ★★★

EVOLUTION: *NO EVOLUTIONS*
FUSION: *NO FUSIONS*

STATS

SKILL: Venocharge

ATTACK: Maul

SOULTIMATE MOVE: Octo snake

INSPIRIT: Venoct's Blessing

TECHNIQUE: Voltage

CATCHPHRASE: "This is my time for revenge."

FAVORITE FOOD: Seafood

EASINESS TO BEFRIEND: —

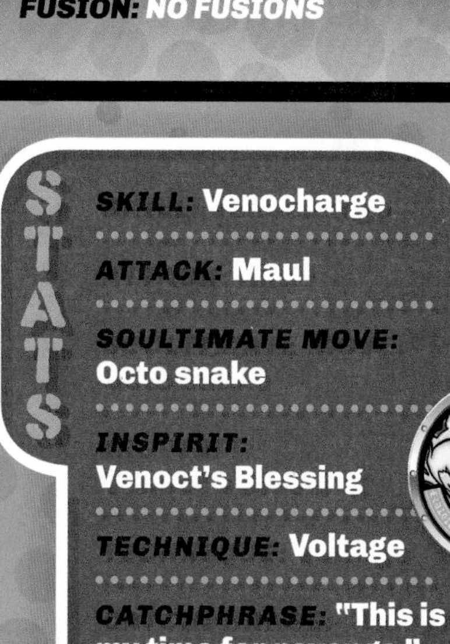

NUMBER 212

SLIPPERY

TV SEASON 2

VENOCT

An elite Yo-kai who fights with his dragon scarf. All of his abilities are truly first class.

EVOLUTION: *NO EVOLUTIONS* ✻ **FUSION:** *NO FUSIONS*

RARE!

SHADOW VENOCT

NUMBER
213

SLIPPERY

RARE! Venoct's shadow, who is skilled in the deadly arts. Few live long after learning that he exists.

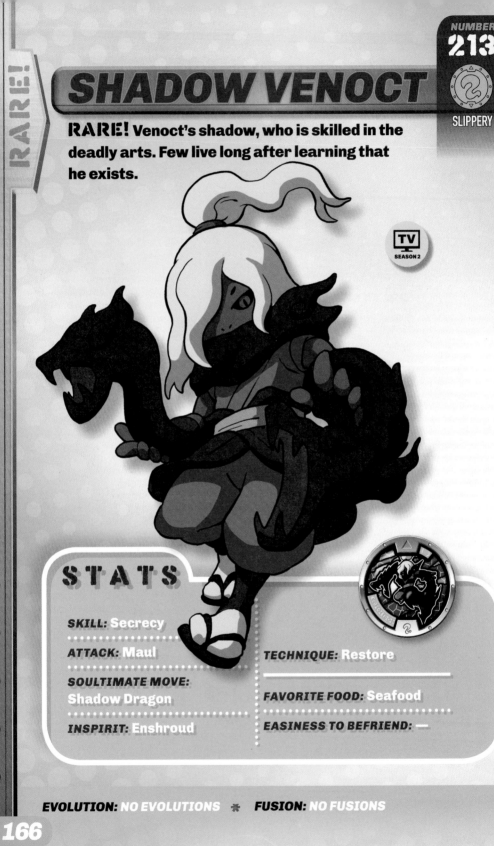

STATS

SKILL: Secrecy

ATTACK: Maul

SOULTIMATE MOVE: Shadow Dragon

INSPIRIT: Enshroud

TECHNIQUE: Restore

FAVORITE FOOD: Seafood

EASINESS TO BEFRIEND: —

EVOLUTION: NO EVOLUTIONS ✱ **FUSION:** NO FUSIONS

NUMBER 214

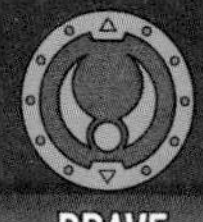

BRAVE

SHOGUNYAN

LEGENDARY!

IN THE VIDEO GAME:

LEGEND! A legendary Jibanyan who became a warrior. He loves skipjack tuna and carries it around in his armor.

IN THE ANIMATION:

When you collect a certain number of Yo-kai Medals, you may unlock a seal that summons a legendary Yo-kai. Shogunyan is one of those Yo-kai. He also reveals that he is Jibanyan's ancestor.

STATS

SKILL: Extreme Critical

ATTACK: Lightning Slash

SOULTIMATE MOVE: Bonito Blade

INSPIRIT: Heart of a Warrior

TECHNIQUE: Storm

CAT-PHRASE: "Ultimate ring-shaped cake-sharing splitter!"

FAVORITE FOOD: Seafood

EASINESS TO BEFRIEND: —

EVOLUTION: NO EVOLUTIONS * **FUSION:** NO FUSIONS

LEGENDARY!

NUMBER
215

MYSTERIOUS

KOMASHURA

LEGEND!

A legendary Komasan with the heart of a greater demon. He scorches his foes with infernal flame.

STATS

SKILL: Blazing Fighting Spirit

ATTACK: Practiced Punch

SOULTIMATE MOVE: Shura Shower

INSPIRIT: Burly Power

TECHNIQUE: Incinerate

FAVORITE FOOD: Milk

EASINESS TO BEFRIEND: —

EVOLUTION: NO EVOLUTIONS * **FUSION:** NO FUSIONS

EERIE

DANDOODLE

LEGENDARY!

IN THE VIDEO GAME:

LEGEND! **A legendary Manjimutt that, through some sort of mistake, got handsome. His smile is so soothing!**

IN THE ANIMATION:

When Nate's Yo-kai Medallium is all filled up, it begins to glow, and Dandoodle shows up. Unlike Manjimutt, he's a legend with the ladies.

STATS

SKILL: Popularity

ATTACK: Tackle

SOULTIMATE MOVE: Handsome Grin

INSPIRIT: Healing Air

TECHNIQUE: Paradise

CATCHPHRASE: "Fabulous!"

FAVORITE FOOD: Chinese Food

EASINESS TO BEFRIEND: —

EVOLUTION: NO EVOLUTIONS ✲ **FUSION:** NO FUSIONS

NUMBER 217

HEARTFUL

ELDER BLOOM

LEGEND! This legendary Hungramps supposedly once filled a city with spirit-invigorating cherry blossoms.

STATS

SKILL: Caring

ATTACK: Headsmack

SOULTIMATE MOVE: Full Bloom

INSPIRIT: Miracle Blossom

TECHNIQUE: Paradise

CATCHPHRASE: "Have a blooming good day!"

FAVORITE FOOD: Rice Balls

EASINESS TO BEFRIEND: —

EVOLUTION: NO EVOLUTIONS * **FUSION:** NO FUSIONS

NUMBER
218

TOUGH

GILGAROS

LEGENDARY!

LEGEND! **The strongest Oni ever born. His power is so great that it needs no explanation. None. At all.**

STATS

SKILL: Extreme Critical

ATTACK: Clobber

SOULTIMATE MOVE: Golden Beatdown

INSPIRIT: Power of Terror

TECHNIQUE: Lightning

FAVORITE FOOD: Meat

EASINESS TO BEFRIEND: —

EVOLUTION: NO EVOLUTIONS * **FUSION:** NO FUSIONS

RARE!

NUMBER 219

SAPPHINYAN

RARE! Jibanyan made of sapphire. His body is the color of a clear ocean on a beautiful summer day.

STATS

SKILL: Linked Together

ATTACK: Sharp Claws

SOULTIMATE MOVE: Pure-Blue Paws

INSPIRIT: Sapphire Power

TECHNIQUE: Waterfall

EASINESS TO BEFRIEND: —

EVOLUTION: NO EVOLUTIONS ✻ **FUSION:** NO FUSIONS

NUMBER
220

CHARMING

EMENYAN

RARE!

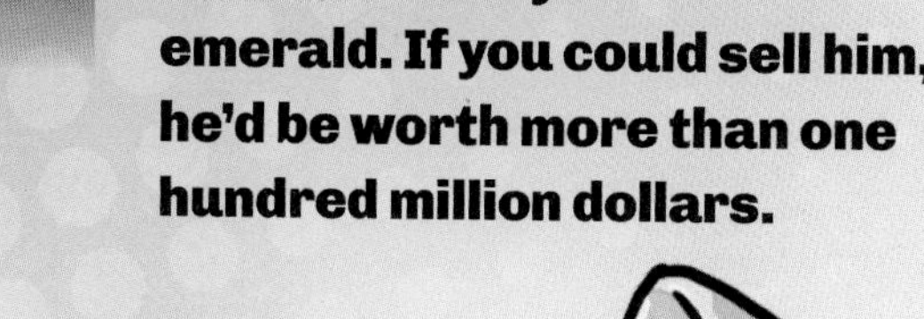

RARE! Jibanyan made of emerald. If you could sell him, he'd be worth more than one hundred million dollars.

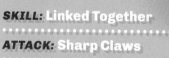

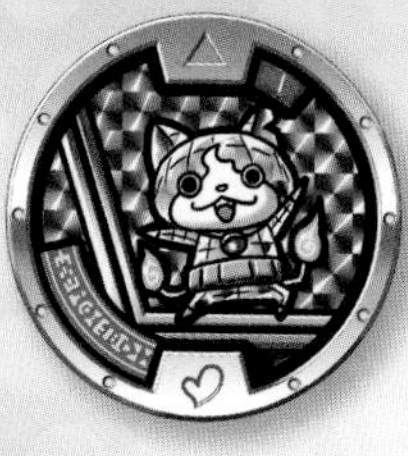

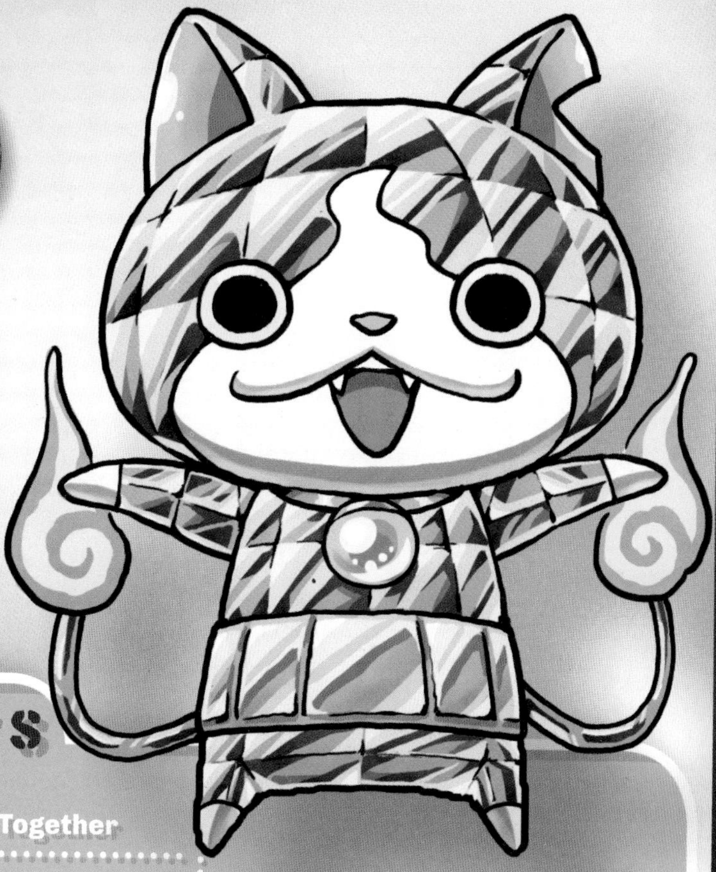

STATS

SKILL: Linked Together

ATTACK: Sharp Claws

TECHNIQUE: Paradise

SOULTIMATE MOVE: Cutie Paws

INSPIRIT: Emerald Power

EASINESS TO BEFRIEND: —

EVOLUTION: NO EVOLUTIONS * **FUSION:** NO FUSIONS

NUMBER
221

RUBINYAN

RARE! Jibanyan made of ruby. Firelike light reflects off him as he fights.

STATS

SKILL: Linked Together

ATTACK: Sharp Claws

TECHNIQUE: Incinerate

SOULTIMATE MOVE: Ruby Boogie

INSPIRIT: Ruby Power

EASINESS TO BEFRIEND: —

EVOLUTION: NO EVOLUTIONS ✱ **FUSION:** NO FUSIONS

NUMBER
222

CHARMING

TOPANYAN

RARE! Jibanyan made of topaz. Making friends with him means you have inherently good luck.

STATS

SKILL: Linked Together

ATTACK: Sharp Claws

SOULTIMATE MOVE: Glittering Paws

INSPIRIT: Topaz Power

TECHNIQUE: Voltage

EASINESS TO BEFRIEND: —

EVOLUTION: NO EVOLUTIONS * **FUSION:** NO FUSIONS

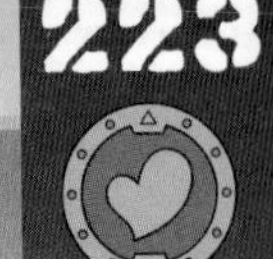

RARE!

NUMBER 223

CHARMING

DIANYAN

TV SEASON 2

RARE! Jibanyan made of diamonds. It's said to be the most lavish, timeless, and romantic Yo-kai. Do you think so? I do!

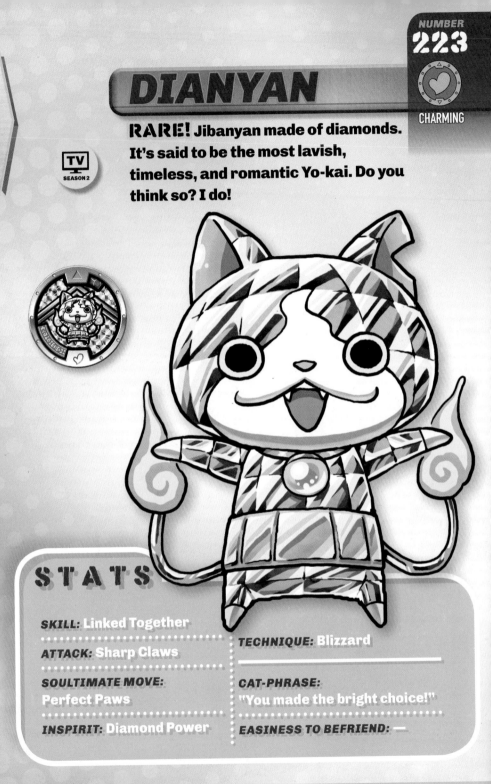

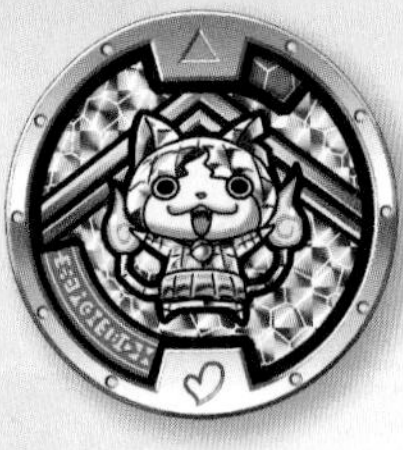

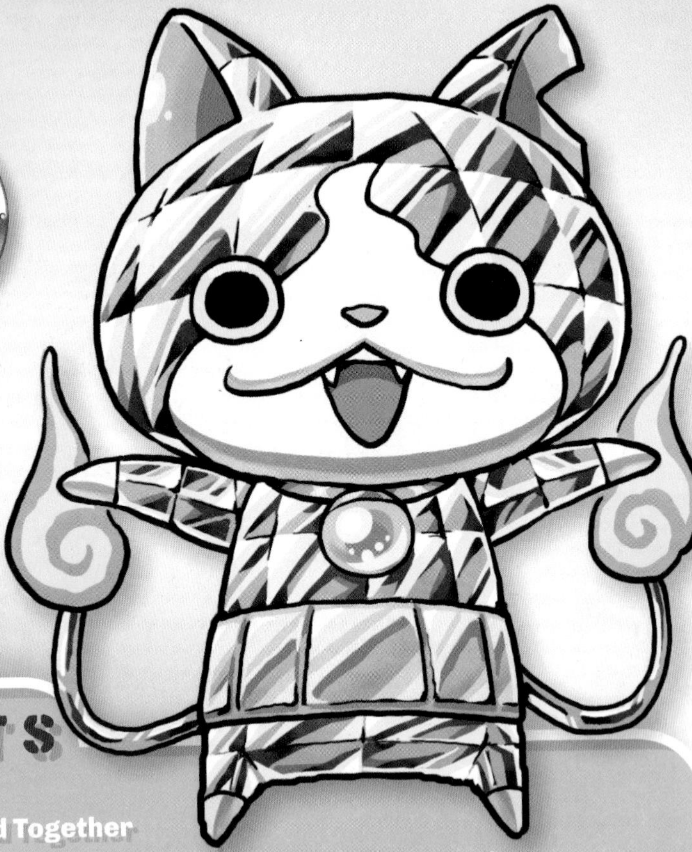

STATS

SKILL: Linked Together

ATTACK: Sharp Claws

SOULTIMATE MOVE: Perfect Paws

INSPIRIT: Diamond Power

TECHNIQUE: Blizzard

CAT-PHRASE: "You made the bright choice!"

EASINESS TO BEFRIEND: —

EVOLUTION: NO EVOLUTIONS * **FUSION:** NO FUSIONS

SLIMAMANDER (SLYMANDER)

A huge snakelike Yo-kai with three big-mouthed heads and skin thicker than an elephant's. Aim for the eye in its mouth!

NUMBER
225

SPROINK

IN THE VIDEO GAME:

This middle-aged Yo-kai loves hot baths and even sneaks into hot springs after hours. He turns red and snorts fire from his nose when he's been soaking too long.

IN THE ANIMATION:

Sproink was hard for Nate and Whisper to get rid of. Blazion and Roughraff both bailed. But an old man who liked his baths lava hot finally made the water too hot for Sproink . . . and everyone else!

NUMBER 226

SV SNAGGERJAG

The guardian spirit of Gourd Pond, he gets mad if he sees anyone mistreating it. The fish respect his manly personality, and they'll do whatever he asks.

NUMBER 227

MASSIFACE

If a giant man-shaped shadow falls over you on a hazy night, DO NOT turn around. Just wait for him to leave. Those who turn around disappear and fade from memory . . .

NUMBER
228

PHANTASMURAI

This eerie suit of armor wanders the museum every night. Or at least that's what the mouse who moves it wants you to think.

NUMBER
229

TARANTUTOR

A spider Yo-kai who lives at school and looks for prime opportunities to eat students. It's too shy to come out during the day, though.

BOSS

DR. MADDIMAN

This madman used to perform experiments at his hospital. Now, as a boss Yo-kai, he is still looking to perform experiments!

NUMBER
231

MCKRAKEN

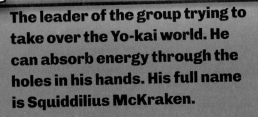

The leader of the group trying to take over the Yo-kai world. He can absorb energy through the holes in his hands. His full name is Squiddilius McKraken.

NUMBER
232

BOSS

MCKRAKEN 2ND FORM

McKraken absorbed the aura that pervaded Springdale and gained monstrous power. He can control the elements and can cause massive destruction.

NUMBER
233

DUWHEEL

The blue, cheery side of Duwheel is always smiling. Don't cross him, or its head will flip upside down and turn an angry shade of red!

NUMBER 234

CHIRPSTER

If you hear music coming from an old, abandoned mansion, this Yo-kai is likely partying there. If you stumble in, you may be dancing till dawn!

NUMBER 235

EYEDRA

A huge salamander Yo-kai who lives in the inferno. Those who fall under its red-eyed gaze cower in fear before being swallowed whole.

He was once a tiny pig Yo-kai, but when he drank some broth he made by boiling other Yo-kai . . . he got huge!

STYX MK. VI

Styx Mk. VI fishes souls out of the River Styx. No sinner escapes his net. On good fishing days, he sings sea shanties that resound through the inferno.

BOSS

NUMBER 238

CLIPSO

This massive being returns to Earth on cloud-covered nights to take away kids who like to stay up all night. Goodnight!

NUMBER 239

DR. NOGUT

A mad doctor Yo-kai whose goal is to create the ideal Yo-kai. He used his own guts in one experiment.

NUMBER
240

BOSS

SPOOKLUNK

This armor once belonged to a strong warrior. It now gathers vassals in the inferno and waits to return to battle someday.

SQUISKER

Sent to the inferno after falling victim to one of his distant relative's schemes, this former politician is filled with a blind rage.

BOSS

NUMBER 242

WOBBLEWOK (POTTERGEIST)

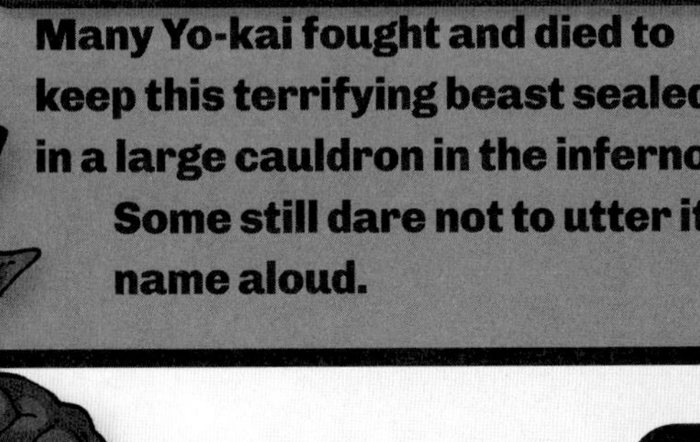

Many Yo-kai fought and died to keep this terrifying beast sealed in a large cauldron in the inferno. Some still dare not to utter its name aloud.

NUMBER 243

TV SEASONS 1 AND 2

GARGAROS

IN THE VIDEO GAME:

A giant red Oni that appears in children's nightmares. Some say it's the essence of childhood fears given full form. If you triumph over this nightmare, you will grow as a person.

IN THE ANIMATION:

Gargaros will chase you down with his club if you leave your house when you're not allowed to. Nate, Whisper, and Jibanyan learned that lesson the day they didn't listen to Nate's mom and snuck out for doughnuts.

NUMBER 244

OGRALUS

Ogralus is said to appear in the dreams of lying children to scare them back to honesty. Liars cannot escape from Ogralus or their nightmares.

NUMBER 245

ORCANOS

Orcanos appears in the nightmares of lazy children and tries to punish them. The fear usually jolts them awake. So now, did you do all of your homework . . .?

INDEX

Looking for a specific Yo-kai? The index below lists all the Yo-kai in this book alphabetically. After each Yo-kai's name, you'll see his or her number. The next number is the page where you'll find the Yo-kai's stats. Happy reading!

Abodabat, #148, 123
Agon, #140, 118
Ake, #138, 116
Alhail, #175, 140
Alloo, #50, 53
Almi, #206, 161
Appak, #97, 87
Armsman, #63, 62
Auntie Heart, #135, 113
Awevil, #161, 132
Azure Dragon, #200, 157
B3-NK1, #20, 34
Babblong, #207, 162
Baddinyan, #95, 85
Badude, #71, 66
Baku, #103, 91
Bananose, #208, 163
Beelzebold, #158, 129
Beetall, #24, 37
Beetler, #23, 37
Belfree, #149, 124
Benkei, #19, 34
Betterfly, #123, 104
Blandon, #145, 121
Blazion, #12, 27
Blips, #36, 45
Blizzaria, #109, 95
Bloominoko, #190, 150
Blowkade, #66, 63
Bruff, #72, 67
Buhu, #166, 135
Cadable, #88, 79
Cadin, #87, 79
Casanono, #42, 48
Casanuva, #41, 48
Castelius I, #78, 71
Castelius II, #77, 70
Castelius III, #76, 70
Castelius Max, #79, 72
Chansin, #15, 30
Chatalie, #177, 142
Cheeksqueek, #180, 143
Chilhuahua, #91, 81
Chippa, #120, 102
Chirpster, #234, 182
Chummer, #203, 159
Clipso, #238, 184
Compunzer, #182, 144
Confuze, #202, 158
Contrarioni, #152, 126
Copperled, #209, 164
Corptain, #11, 26
Coughkoff, #162, 133
Count Cavity, #159, 130
Croonger, #193, 152
Cruncha, #25, 38
Cupistol, #40, 47
Cutta-nah, #4, 22

Cutta-nah-nah, #5, 22
Cuttincheez, #181, 144
Cynake, #210, 164
Daiz, #201, 158
Damona, #110, 96
Dandoodle, #216, 169
Darumacho, #58, 58
Dazzabel, #84, 77
Dianyan, #223, 176
Dimmy, #144, 121
Dismarelda, #179, 143
Dr. Maddiman, #230, 180
Dr. Nogut, #239, 184
Draggie, #198, 156
Dragon Lord, #199, 156
Drizzle, #173, 139
Dromp, #82, 75
Droplette, #172, 139
Dubbles, #131, 111
Duchoo, #29, 41
Dulluma, #57, 58
Dummkap, #31, 42
Duwheel, #233, 181
D'wanna, #32, 43
Elder Bloom, #217, 170
Elloo, #49, 52
Emenyan, #220, 173
Enefly, #122, 103
Enerfly, #121, 103
Espy, #51, 53
Eterna, #186, 147
Everfore, #185, 146
Eyedra, #235, 182
Fidgephant, #64, 62
Fishpicable, #195, 153
Flengu, #54, 55
Flumpy, #167, 135
Frostail, #56, 57
Frostina, #108, 95
Gargaros, #243, 186
Gilgaros, #218, 171
Gleam, #18, 33
Goldenyan, #81, 74
Goruma, #59, 59
Grainpa, #118, 101
Greesel, #160, 131
Grubsnitch, #115, 99
Grumples, #184, 145
Gush, #176, 141
Happierre, #125, 106
Heheheel, #192, 152
Helmsman, #9, 25
Hidabat, #147, 122
Hoggles, #236, 183
Hornaplenty, #75, 69
Hungorge, #117, 100
Hungramps, #116, 100
Hurchin, #163, 133
Illoo, #48, 52
Impass, #61, 60
Infour, #52, 54
Insomni, #187, 148
Jibanyan, #93, 83
Kapunki, #22, 36
Komajiro, #101, 90
Komane, #100, 90

INDEX

Komasan, #99, 89
Komashura, #215, 168
Komiger, #102, 91
Kyubi, #55, 56
Lafalotta, #35, 45
Lamedian, #183, 145
Lava Lord, #69, 65
Leadoni, #136, 114
Ledballoon, #67, 64
Lodo, #119, 102
Mad Mountain, #68, 64
Mama Aura, #134, 113
Manjimutt, #169, 137
Massiface, #227, 178
McKraken, #231, 180
McKraken (2nd Form), #232, 181
Minochi, #8, 24
Mirapo, #46, 51
Mircle, #47, 51
Mochismo, #7, 24
Moskevil, #142, 119
Multimutt, #170, 137
Mynimo, #137, 115
Nagatha, #178, 142
Negasus, #155, 127
Negatibuzz, #141, 119
Neighfarious, #156, 128
Nird, #154, 127
N'more, #33, 43
Noko, #189, 150
Noway, #60, 59
Nul, #146, 122
Ogralus, #244, 187
Ol' Fortune, #129, 109
Ol' Saint Trick, #128, 108
Orcanos, #245, 187
Pandanoko, #191, 151
Pandle, #1, 20
Papa Bolt, #132, 111
Payn, #139, 117
Peckpocket, #164, 134
Peppillon, #124, 105
Phantasmurai, #228, 179
Pinkipoo, #106, 93
Pookivil, #107, 94
Pupsicle, #90, 81
Quaken, #13, 28
Q'wit, #34, 44
Rageon, #196, 154
Rattelle, #85, 77
Reuknight, #10, 25
Reversa, #126, 106
Reversette, #127, 107
Rhinoggin, #73, 68
Rhinormous, #74, 68
Rhyth, #113, 98
Robonyan, #80, 73
Rockabelly, #165, 134
Rollen, #130, 110
Roughraff, #70, 65
Rubinyan, #221, 174
Sandi, #188, 149
Sapphinyan, #219, 172
Scritchy, #143, 120
Shadow Venoct, #213, 166

Sheen, #16, 31
Shmoopie, #105, 93
Shogunyan, #214, 167
Shrook, #204, 159
Signibble, #43, 49
Signiton, #44, 49
Singcada, #89, 80
Sir Berus, #171, 138
Siro, #14, 29
Skelebella, #86, 78
Skranny, #39, 47
Skreek, #168, 136
Slacka-slash, #6, 23
Slimamander, (Slymander), #224, 177
Slitheref, #211, 165
Slush, #174, 140
Snartle, #27, 40
Snee, #17, 32
Snotsolong, #28, 41
Spenp, #205, 160
Spooklunk, #240, 185
Sproink, #225, 177
Squisker, #241, 185
Statiking, #45, 50
Steppa, #112, 97
Styx Mk. VI, #237, 183
Supyo, #98, 88
Sushiyama, #21, 35
Suspicioni, #150, 125
SV Snaggerjag, #226, 178
Swelterrier, #92, 82
Swosh, #83, 76
Tanbo, #3, 21
Tantroni, #151, 125
Tarantutor, #229, 179
Tattlecast, #38, 46
Tattletell, #37, 46
Tengloom, #153, 126
Tengu, #53, 54
Thornyan, #94, 84
Timidevil, #157, 129
Topanyan, #222, 175
Touphant, #65, 63
Tunatic, #197, 155
Uncle Infinite, #133, 112
Undy, #2, 20
Urnaconda, #194, 153
Venoct, #212, 165
Walkappa, #96, 86
Walldin, #62, 61
Wantston, #114, 98
Wazzat, #30, 42
Whapir, #104, 92
Wiglin, #111, 97
Wobblewok (Pottergeist), #242, 186
Zerberker, #26, 39

SEE YOU NYEXT TIME!